WINTER BURN

WINTER BURN

Jacqueline Druga

PRESS

Published by Vulpine Press in the United Kingdom in 2022

ISBN: 978-1-83919-474-0

www.vulpine-press.com

For my grandchildren, Aiden and Mia, who followed and trusted me, without question, into the cold, deep belly and bowels of Laurel Caverns so I could research this book.

ONE

THE BROTHER

No one ever says to you, "Oh, that sucks." It's always, "I'm sorry or that's terrible to hear", something along those lines.

The polite version of what they're thinking, but just unable to say.

I was guilty of the same thing.

I'd hear bad news, think it sucked but never say so. After everything, I think I'll start a social media campaign to replace the 'sorry' and 'condolences' with 'it sucks.'

Three siblings. Three of us. And one was dying.

Not old enough to vote, or fight for his country, my older brother Sean was fighting for his life.

And it sucked.

He was never uber popular, didn't play sports or shine as some sort of all-star, at least not until everyone found out he was sick. Just average, never stood out. A good guy. Then suddenly he was homecoming king, and everyone wanted to be the dying boy's friend.

I hated them all. The fake cheerleading captain in her pink gown coming to our house to take pictures with the sick kid.

I was so mad, but my mom was like, "Allie...stop."

Fine. I'd stop. For Sean's sake.

One year older than me, we acted like twins, and like most twins, personality wise, we were opposite of each other. He was nice, I was stubborn. He was funny ... I wasn't.

We both swore to make sure our youngest brother, Josh was like neither of us. He was in eighth grade, but still formidable.

Our family dynamic was good.

Normal fights, fun times when it was boring.

Then a simple pain in his neck turned into a diagnosis no one expected.

Everything changed.

It changed so fast.

At first, they though Sean had injured it during gym class or something like that. But that wasn't the case.

The tumor was part of his spinal system.

It spread fast affecting his ability to walk, move his arms or even feed himself.

The treatments didn't just take his hair, they sucked away what little body weight he had.

They didn't, however, take away his spirit.

He went from sharing a room with Josh to being in a hospital bed in the small dining area of a two-bedroom apartment.

We used to have a house.

Not even a month after Sean's diagnosis, things got worse. My mom had to quit her job, my father changed his to be more accessible and the insurance didn't cover anything.

My parents sold the house.

I understood. Anything to get my brother what he needed.

Still, I didn't believe he was dying.

Not yet.

A good old Christmas present from the doctor gave Sean six more months.

It was the worst Christmas ever. Sean joked that he would at least be around long enough to graduate.

Not funny. And I didn't believe that it was going to happen. He wasn't dying. Not yet.

My parents did all that they could. Trying to pretend we didn't go from middle class to poor. Like I didn't see my mother whipping out that food benefit card. Did she really think I cared about that? Like we were the only kids in school who got free lunches? Did she think me or Josh cared about having less presents? Or that we no longer had a backyard in a quiet home, trading it for screaming upstairs neighbors and a building frequented by police.

No. None of that mattered. Adjustments had to be made in our life. They were minor compared to what Sean faced.

I would trade anything and everything for him not to die.

TWO

THE MOTHER

In the winter, I saw the first real positive aspect to living in an apartment complex.

Snow.

No one arguing about who would shovel the driveway or walk.

There was no need. The guys at the apartment complex did it all.

It was disappointing though; all that snow and we were still on winter break. No snow day or cyber day. It was almost like a rip off. New Years fell on a Wednesday so no reason to send us back to school two days before the weekend.

New Year's Eve came without fanfare for us. Although we could hear throughout the apartment building people shouting, cheering, banging pots, we didn't really do anything big. Just the five of us watching whatever station we could with that digital antenna my dad bought. Yelling out Happy New Year when the clock struck midnight. We didn't have cable and it was like an unspoken rule that everyone used the Wi-Fi of the property manager.

There were times we just were so behind in everything.

You never realize how important internet and cable are until you don't have them and you miss the news stories that people talk about in school. We did have our phones, but the data and speed on those weren't always the best.

It was frustrating waiting for a page to load.

Sometimes it felt old fashioned, like I was my parents in a time when they either didn't have internet or they used the phone line.

The night of the first of the year brought the first major snowstorm of winter. Of course, it was a surprise to us, we didn't have cable so we didn't catch the local weather report.

But being in Pennsylvania, the blanket of snow was cleared from the streets pretty fast.

My mom was happy about that. She wanted to go to the grocery store at some point. The food we bought for the holidays had dwindled away to leftovers we picked at. A ham that dried out and pork and sauerkraut that just smelled gross.

My father told her she could go the next day, but she couldn't. She had to go into Pittsburgh to get medication for my brother that the Uniontown pharmacies didn't have.

So after we knew the snow had slowed down enough, and the roads were truly passable, I ventured out with my mother to the grocery store.

Of course, unlike when we had a house, we didn't just walk out the door to the car sitting in the driveway, the automatic starter having it ready and warm.

If we pre-started our car in our complex there was a good chance it would be gone by the time we stepped outside.

We spent fifteen minutes clearing the car and digging it out. The plow that came through the parking lot just blocked us in with snow.

Finally we pulled out and headed to the store. My mother talked a lot about going to Pittsburgh and how she hated making the drive alone.

I thought it was a hint for me to go, but I wasn't taking that bait. I hated the drive there, especially the traffic as we got closer to the city.

"Why don't you ask Dad to go," I suggested. "He's off on Fridays."

"I can't leave you alone with Sean."

"Why not? You'll only be gone a couple hours and you two never go anywhere together."

"Allie, I can't leave you to take care of your brother."

"Yeah, you can. I can do it," I replied. "I have all the numbers and I stayed with him before when you guys went Christmas shopping."

"That was different."

"How I asked."

"We were close to home."

"It's not different, Mom."

Then she did that parent thing and said, "I'll think about it."

I never knew if she actually thought about anything she told me she'd think about. Mainly because when she said, "I'll think about it", her answer was always no.

Taking care of my brother wasn't a big deal whether she was two miles away or sixty. I was capable and everything would be fine.

Little did I know so much was about to change in such a small time frame.

THREE

SHOPPER VALUE

The first sign that something was wrong was in the parking lot of the grocery store. It was jammed packed and people drove kind of crazy trying to get a spot.

Two people actually raced by my mother taking the spot she was trying to get.

"This is insane," my mother said, "Allie, check your phone. See if we're having another storm."

Ah, yes, the snowpocalypse shoppers. The people that went out for bread, milk and toilet paper at the slightest inkling of bad weather.

My father was always funny about them, yet he was out there buying stuff with them.

I pulled up the weather app and saw flurries, but nothing major.

"No."

"This is odd. There has to be a major storm coming," she said. "Has to be."

We finally found a spot, way in the back. I thought ahead and grabbed the first empty cart I saw as we passed. It was a good thing, there were none in the front of the store nor inside.

There were four check-out lanes, and two police officers stood at the bottom. I wondered why they were there and then I saw.

The cashier took one of the gallons of milk from a man's cart. "The limit is one sir."

"I have four kids," the man replied.

"I'm sorry, that's the rule so there's enough for everyone."

The man was upset, but he accepted that rule. I supposed there were people that didn't and that was why the police had to be there.

The fresh produce had been picked over and nothing was left, which made me laugh because how long would that last if people were stranded in their houses?

I had never seen the shelves so bare, and signs were everywhere, limiting how many of an item a customer could take.

"Honestly, this is crazy." My mother finally pulled out her phone. "What the hell is going on in..." her words trailed off.

"Mom?"

"Um...nothing." She shook her head, tucking her phone back in her purse.

"Another storm?"

"Yes. Tomorrow."

"It must be bad," I said. "You look worried. Maybe you should wait until Monday to get Sean's medication."

"No. No now I can't. I really can't," she rattled nervously. "He has very little left and…The storm isn't supposed to come until afternoon. We'll be fine." She rested her hand on mine as I pushed the cart. "Let's get what we can."

We were two in hordes of people in that store, pushing and shoving for what they could get off the shelf.

A simple trip took us nearly two hours and my mother remained in some sort of quiet, shocked state.

Her behavior was so off, it was hard to believe it was over a snowstorm.

It had to be more and she just wasn't telling.

FOUR

THIN WALLS

I wasn't sure when it happened, just at some point it did. My parents made the choice to filter what they told us, protect us from the truth or possibly just tweak it some.

It was okay to tell me my brother was sick, but they didn't really get into what was wrong with him.

It was fine to tell me that they had to give up the house, they just failed to tell me why we lost the house in a month and suddenly my parents were earning so little that we qualified for food and housing benefits.

Neither of them worked much.

I probably turned a blind eye to everything.

After talking to my friend Sarah, she explained that maybe my parents lost their jobs over Sean. Maybe he was going to be sick a lot longer. They didn't want me to worry.

It didn't matter to me that we were poor, I just wished my mother would realize that I was a lot more mature than she gave me credit for. A maturity that came rather fast after our lives changed. Did I want to be? No. I wanted to be a teenage girl worried about what I would wear, who I would hang out with and where I'd go with my friends.

Instead, I worried that I would miss a moment with my brother.

Every trip to the mall, the movies or just hanging out, I wouldn't miss when I turned thirty, but time with my brother, if I missed that, it was something I would regret.

I didn't have much time left with him.

If the apartment wasn't so small, I'd feel bad that his bed was in the dining room. It wasn't much of a dining room, though.

Actually, my parents switched the dining and living areas. The entrance of our apartment had a short hallway with a closet to the right that had the small water heater. That hall led into a big room. The front part was the living room, at the other end was the dining area, complete with a hanging ceiling fan.

The kitchen was small. A partial open concept with only a counter separating the eating area from the cooking area.

We moved the couch there so Sean not only could see out the big window of the living room, but didn't need to be so close to cooking smells.

The hallway to the two bedrooms was off the kitchen. Me and Josh shared a room. Two twin beds crammed in a really small bedroom.

We also took turns sleeping on the sofa. Neither of us minded, it gave us space.

When I slept out there, I spent a lot of time listening to Sean's breathing.

Then again, Sean would talk a lot to which ever one of us spent the night out there.

It was an older apartment. Government subsidy. At one time I suppose it was modern. It wasn't bad and didn't look like something fifty years old.

But the walls were thin and I could hear my parents argue.

They didn't fight much and they never yelled, but they spoke in these intense low volume voice which travelled as much in the middle of the night as if they were screaming.

"I got as much as I could," my mother said. "There wasn't much there. Ask Allie."

"I believe you, but couldn't you have gone to another store?" my dad asked.

"No. No. It was crazy out there. I just wanted to get home. We'll make do."

"For how long? How long will it last?"

"Not long enough to run out of what we have, I'm sure."

"I worry about water," my Dad said. "No power. No utilities."

"I've been reading about it since I heard. The last time something like this happened, it knocked out power for a few days. We'll be fine. I just need to make sure we get Sean's meds. That's all."

"I hate leaving the kids."

"Do you want to stay back?" she asked.

"No. I'd rather you didn't go alone."

What in the world were they talking about? A snowstorm so big that it was going to knock out power for days? My father worried about water, but what about heat? It was below zero outside.

I sought out my tablet and quietly left my bedroom. I needed to try to get a Wi-Fi signal.

As I entered the living room, I saw the glow of Sean's eBook reader against his face.

"Can't sleep?" he asked.

"I wanted to look something up," I held up my tablet. "I need Wi-Fi."

"Try Ziggy's, it's the strongest."

"Thanks," I opened up my settings. "Are you okay? Do you need anything?"

"I'm fine. I wish mom and dad would stop arguing."

"About the weather."

"Seriously?" asked Sean.

"Yeah. I guess there's a super bad storm supposed to hit tomorrow, that's what I want to look up. What's the Ziggy password this month."

"Fullmoon12345678."

I laughed, "Not original."

I looked at the available internet connections. It was funny. Most families paid a small fortune for internet, while we, like a lot of people in the building, paid the maintenance guy ten bucks a month for passwords to various internet accounts in the building, including the rental agent. We had four this month. Sometimes we only had three. Whatever the maintenance man could get, he sold.

I heard my brother chuckle softly and I glanced from my tablet to him. He was reading something funny. I loved to hear him laugh. When he got out of control, he cackled, then snorted. Sometimes when I looked at him, he didn't seem sick at all. His coloring would be good, his eyes not so dark, then other days he looked so worn, he could have passed for a boxer with his black eyes.

"Ziggy connected," I reported.

"Not sure why you didn't just use your phone for the weather. You have that app on the home screen."

"I did. It didn't say anything about a storm. Just cold." I opened the browser. "Maybe the weather channel is behind or something."

"Just go local."

"That's what I'm doing. I figure..." My hand froze, hovering about the screen as the local news site loaded. I didn't need to press 'weather' or even search. What frightened my mother was there, right on the front page of the news. "Sean."

"Huh?"

"It's not snow."

"What isn't?" he asked.

"The storm warning that scared mom." I walked over to him with the tablet. "Look. It's not a snowstorm they're warning about."

Sean took the tablet. "It's a solar storm."

"Yeah. I'm not sure what that is."

"It's nothing." Sean returned my tablet. "I mean it's not nothing, but it's not such a big deal that people empty the store shelves."

"You don't think?"

"No. They happen all the time. Who am I though? You have the world at your fingertips. See what you can find."

"I will…" I grabbed the tablet and made my way near the window for a better signal. Sean was probably right. He was pretty smart. But on the outside chance he was wrong, I wanted to learn more. I needed to know what it was about this storm that had everyone panicking.

FIVE

SWITCHING UP

There are generally two types of truths when searching for answers on the internet. The kind that scientists answer, where respectable news sources publish them or, well, forums or conspiracy sites.

One end of the spectrum said it was nothing to worry about. That at most, there would be some power outages, though this was not likely, and the radiation would be no more than an x ray.

The other end was like "bring on the apocalypse".

It was extreme and I didn't want to be around if all that happened.

Blackouts, high levels of radiation, solar winds that would fry everything like a nuclear blast.

It seemed a bit much, so my logic was to find a middle ground.

That middle ground still had us in danger.

I worried about Sean, but at least he didn't rely on any electronic machines to keep him alive. He and I talked about it through the night. I even woke Josh to discuss things. It was late, nearly four in the morning, but we didn't have school.

It reminded me so much of when we were really little. The Christmas tree was still up and the lights lit the room.

Although waking Josh wasn't the best idea.

He was a nervous kid.

"Wait, what? A solar storm?" Josh asked. "Why does that not sound good?"

"It's not," I said.

"It could be fine," said Sean.

"No." Josh shook his head. "I hear solar storm and I think, whoa, we're done."

Sean rolled his eyes. "And so does everyone else. Hence why the grocery stores were so packed."

"The grocery stores were packed?" Josh asked.

I nodded. "Barely anything was left."

"Is that why mom didn't get the Goldfish crackers."

"Probably."

Sean laughed.

"What?" I asked.

"His priorities in the apocalypse," Sean replied.

"It's the apocalypse?" Josh asked, panicked.

"Yes," I answered.

"No," Sean said. "It's not but…maybe together, we should think about the 'just in case' and come up with a plan."

And we did. It freaked out my little brother a bit, but together we determined that the biggest threat would be the radiation.

Sean joked that he's been through radiation. I didn't think that was funny.

Radiation was carried through the sun, the ultraviolet rays, so avoiding them would be best.

Therein came the problem. We were no longer in our two story, three-bedroom house on Bell Street. We didn't have a basement. There was only one option.

The hallway or....

My mother huffed as she stood in the doorway. "Allie, why is Sean fully clothed in the bathtub."

The bathroom.

It was a small, interior, windowless room in our apartment.

Not only was my brother in the tub, but we had water and some food, along with candles and the only flashlight my family owned.

"I'm just keeping him safe from the solar storm."

My mother folded her arms. "A huh, and um, why the bathroom?"

"It's the only place I could think of to protect from radiation."

"You realize this solar storm isn't coming until this afternoon, right?"

"It might come earlier," I said. "It's the sun. You know right that whatever is hitting us already left the sun.":

My mother nodded.

"I did my research, Mom," I told her. "Last night. Both me and Sean."

"Are you encouraging this, Sean?" my mother asked him.

"I'm going with the flow," Sean replied.

"Well, I did my research, too," my mother said. "Everyone is overreacting."

"I'm worried," I told her. "I don't want to take chances with Sean. Me and Josh, we can run for cover. This is the best we can do."

Again, she nodded. "So you're concerned?"

"Yes."

"Then I think your father should stay here."

"That's fine but you shouldn't go alone," I told her. "You need someone with you."

"In case the worst happens?" she asked.

"Yes."

"Then good thing I'll have you. Since you are a solar survivor guru all of a sudden."

"Wait. What?" I stood. "Me?"

"Yeah, dad will stay here and you and will head to Pittsburgh. Think of it as mother-daughter bonding." She turned and walked out.

She was so smug about it and so was Sean who started to laugh.

"It's not funny," I snapped.

"Yeah, it is. Mom sucks at driving."

I mumbled under my breath that she sucked at conversation as well. I hated going anywhere with my mother. I mean, I had just gone on that harrowing grocery store trip with her. That was enough for a month. I swore she thought I was still nine years old the way she treated me.

Hopefully my father would pull the macho card and override her decision to take me. But if I had to go, if I absolutely had to go, I was going to be prepared.

SIX

THE FLASH

"Allie, you're ridiculous."

Those were my mother's words to me when I got in the truck.

I was ridiculous.

That was the start of the hour plus trip. Yeah, it was going to be fun.

Did she not remember that the day before she was pretending not to be scared after she saw the news? Did she forget how worried she was? Then all of a sudden, she wasn't.

Apparently she researched the opposite stories to me.

She wasn't worried.

I was scared to death.

My over inflated bookbag was what caused her to make that comment.

Ridiculous.

Okay, yes, so I took some food from the house, a few bottles of water, my favorite throw blanket and a few other things and stuffed them in the bag. A bag I kept on the floor of the car right at my feet.

If we didn't need them, so what?

But what if we did?

Everything seemed normal driving to the city. The roads weren't empty. People didn't seem to care that some sort of major event was about to happen. There was a homeless guy standing off to the side of the road, waiting for traffic to slow down so he could get help.

His sign said he needed food. I was going to give him a can of SPAM, but my mother gave him a dollar and I gave him a little bag of chips.

I did so with an apologetic look, because I did wish we had more.

He looked grateful for that single bill, telling us, "Bless you," as he smiled.

The homeless guy wasn't young, but he wasn't old either.

I looked at his shoes as he walked away.

My friend Jessie said if they have good shoes, they don't need the money.

I didn't believe that because I was certain organizations passed out shoes and coats to the homeless.

In any event, I still looked at his torn and tattered shoes.

My mother didn't give him a second glance.

It was a normal day.

A part of me even thought that my mother was dismissing it, stating she wanted to get out of the city and across the river before rush hour traffic and you can only get hit with something from the sun when it's daylight.

That was a valid point. Whether it was true or not, I didn't know.

We were on the eastern part of the country, if it didn't come early, it would be dark when it arrived.

After getting Sean's medicine from the hospital, we headed back home. There was some traffic on the bridge, not much, so we moved at a slow pace. The bridge led to the Liberty Tunnels. They were nearly a mile long and would take is directly to Route 51 South, the four-lane road we needed to take home.

Once we hit that, it would be smooth sailing.

But the tunnel was congested and we barely moved.

I just wanted to get home.

I worried about Sean, I just didn't want to be separated from my family. Granted, I was with my mother, but I think we were in that awkward relationship stage that most mothers and teenage daughters hit.

Everything I said she thought was wrong or snippy and everything she said I thought was just embarrassing and annoying.

Like the conversation she chose to have when we ended up coming to a dead stop in the tunnel. We were in the middle, caught in the section where I couldn't see the entrance of the exit.

A tunnel with no end.

Much like my talks with my mother.

"I wonder if it's too late in the day to get an everything bagel," she said.

"Is there a time frame in which you can eat bagels?"

"Don't be so snide."

"I was trying to be funny."

"It wasn't."

"Whatever." I shrugged.

24

My mother huffed. "Anyhow, I was just wondering. They run out of the good ones early at Bagel Mart. Did you ever have one?"

I wanted to tell her, 'Yeah, I have. I hate them.' But not wanting to chance having her snap at me, I just nodded.

"Did you want to stop and see?" she asked. "We'll pass Bagel Mart after the traffic."

"Mom, you know there's like an emergency warning?"

"I do. And if the world ends, I would be able to say I had one last bagel before I died."

"Yeah, well, I want to have a cigarette."

"Allie, you don't smoke do you?" she asked with a slight scold.

"No. But if the world's gonna end I'll be able to say I had one before I died." I paused. "Wait is that an oxymoron?"

"No, I think it's more paradoxical or ironic. Oh ..." my mother breathed out in relief. "We're moving finally."

"Maybe there was an accident."

"Could have been."

We went from a dead stop to moving about fifteen miles per hour and it felt like we were flying. Soon we could see the proverbial light at the end of the tunnel.

Had we been sitting in there so long that the sunlight at the end looked super bright?

"Wow, it got really sunny," my mother said.

Immediately, I knew what it was, and it wasn't a sunny day.

Without a choice, we were emerging from the safety of the deep tunnel into the event that was predicted to change the world.

The same event my mother had started to doubt.

Coming out of that tunnel was like stepping into an over-exposed photograph, everything was so bright. My mother didn't say a word, but her actions spoke volumes to me that she was suddenly worried.

Placing on her turn signal she shifted into the right lane cutting off a minivan to get to the ramp that would take us to Route 51.

My eyes shifted then stayed on the tiny temperature number next to the clock on the radio.

The number increased. It was a cold day when we left, I remember seeing the temperature was twenty-two degrees.

One minute out of the tunnel it read fifty.

"Mom. The temperature is rising."

"What is it?" she asked.

"Fifty-four, sixty-six, it's rising fast."

"That can't be right."

"No, Mom it can't be. It's saying eighty degrees." I wound down my window and I felt the heat come in.

And then after we made that ramp, just about on that road…everything stopped.

The digital readout on the radio went black as the car died, and it wasn't just ours.

I could hear my mom pumping the brakes to slow down the coast. We finally stopped inches before hitting another car, but it didn't stop the car behind us from rear ending us.

It wasn't a bad jolt, after all, he was just drifting as well.

That collision sent us into the car ahead of us, the one we tried to avoid hitting.

I could hear the fender benders everywhere.

Bang-bang-bang-bang.

"Are you okay?" my mother asked me. "Are you hurt?"

"I'm fine. You?"

"Fine." Her hands clutched the steering wheel as she breathed heavily. "This must ... this must be what they were talking about. You know the power outages,"

"Cars, too?"

"Yeah, they called it something, I'm not sure. Didn't you see something about it in all those conspiracy sites?"

"I think so. I paid more attention to the other stuff."

"Well, I'm sure that other stuff won't happen. Look, the brightness is toning down."

She was right, it wasn't quite as overexposed as it was a few minutes earlier. Whatever it was just blasted us with a brightness and cut the power to everything.

Or so we thought.

"We just..." My mother turned the key as if it would suddenly work. "We have to find a way home; I don't think this is going to start."

"How far are we?" I asked.

"Forty miles."

"Can we call someone?"

An intense look of worry swept over my mother's face when she lifted her phone. The screen was black. She pressed the buttons to try to start it.

Nothing.

I pulled out mine.

It was off as well.

As I reached down for my bag, I glanced out of the windshield.

Around us people were getting out of their cars, shucking their winter coats and I could see on my mother's face the debate on whether we should or not.

Stay in the car or get out. Not that we could accomplish anything by staying in the car.

We were just sitting there when suddenly the people, who had been meandering around confused, started running.

I looked at my mother.

Oblivious to anything, I jolted when someone banged on my window.

It was the homeless guy from earlier.

"Get out of the car!" he shouted, even slightly muffled from the glass, I could hear him. "Get out!"

For a split second, just a split second, I thought it was like a case of road rage. But then it struck me that people were running.

He was pointing at something and trying to open my door.

"Allie, we need to go," my mother said rushed.

"What is it?"

Her voice screeched as she shouted, opening her door. "Now! We have run."

What did she see that I didn't? I grabbed my bag, opened the door and all I heard was screaming, then the homeless man just yanked me out.

"Hurry." He pulled me.

As I followed his lead I glanced over my shoulder.

Behind us, ribbons of white and blue swirled violently like rapid flames, they made a high pitch roaring sound and grew rapidly closer. Whatever it was seemed to consume everything in its path.

SEVEN

FIZZLE

It could have been a scene from an old monster movie, the way people ran and screamed, continuously looking back. The adrenaline of the moment caused everything to blur, but I ran. The weight of my bag was bouncing in my momentum and the homeless man had a death grip on my arm.

I couldn't see my mother and I was being pulled faster than I thought I could run.

There were buildings to the right. I guess people were trying to take cover.

The first building was one of those huge storage warehouses. People were crushing each other to get in there. They broke windows in the next building, which was a thrift store, and some long red brick building next to that.

It didn't make sense to break windows, but did it even make sense to even try to run and take cover?

Was it all in vain?

Homeless guy didn't say much in that moment, focusing on getting me somewhere, I was still running forward when he yanked me again, taking me to the right.

I thought we were gonna try to get into the huge thrift store or the other building. I didn't know how we'd manage that.

So many people were clamoring to get inside.

Where was my mother?

She had to be nearby, somewhere behind us. I didn't look.

I prayed she was running with us.

My heart pounded in my chest, I didn't have time to lose my breath. Instead of going to one of the two building, he pulled be through an overgrown small parking lot that ran between the two buildings. The ground was uneven, my feet weren't sturdy.

Where were we going?

"We have to get inside," Homeless guy said. "I think we have to take shelter."

We didn't even know what we were running from and his stating that he 'thought' we needed to take shelter really nailed it.

No one knew.

I didn't.

It could have been nothing and we all ran like idiots.

My first thought was that if we really needed to get inside, then why did we run beyond the buildings?

His route took us down a small grade and then when we reached the bottom we turned right once more.

We raced across a parking lot back toward the thrift store, only now we were behind it, in the back at the basement level. A huge truck was parked there nearly against the building. Still holding me within his clutches, homeless man hurriedly squeezed with me between the space of the truck and the bricks of the building.

It was then that I felt my hand grabbed and I looked over my shoulder.

My mother was with us.

It was a tight squeeze and it all happened so fast.

After scaling the wall with our backs, he pushed open a door. An old wooden one with a boarded-up window.

"Inside," he said. "Go."

I ran in, then my mother.

He closed the door. "Get to the deep corner," he instructed.

Then as if he had done it a million time, he slid an old dresser over the door to block it.

My mother held on to me as we scooted back.

We didn't know what was happening, why we were hiding or taking shelter. Shelter from what?

And why was this man helping us? Surely the bag of Lays potato chips and dollar bill wasn't that life changing?

Maybe he was a psycho and we blindly followed him to our deaths.

I was scared of many things in that moment. It was total blackness. I felt like we were in a dark concrete bunker. No windows, no light. My eyes fought to adjust. I couldn't even see him.

Then I heard this clicking sound. It was followed by a small bluish light that brightened the room a little. It was hand crank lantern.

Holding it up, he inched towards us, his eyes gazing to the ceiling. There wasn't much to see. But we could hear. Muffled footsteps and crying, no discernable words or voices. Just the sound of chaos.

Rumbling voices and movement.

"What's happening?" my mother asked.

He shook his head.

"Maybe nothing?" I stated. "Maybe it's nothing."

Then something happened.

At that second, we didn't know what it was.

Above our heads the rumbling sound of rushing footsteps was followed by a huge crescendo of horrified screams. Screams that were cut short like the power.

In an instant.

Done.

From deafeningly loud to complete silence in a snap of a finger.

EIGHT

IN THE SILENCE

There wasn't a single noise. Nothing coming from above us. The three of us stood there, looking up to the ceiling as if suddenly some answer would swoop down at us.

I know I listened, I listened to hear anything, but there wasn't anything to hear.

There was however this weird smell, like burning rubber. And it was warmer. So much so, I took off my coat.

"What happened?" my mother asked.

Homeless man answered. "I think they're all dead."

My mother gasped.

Really? I thought. Did she really not think everyone was killed?

I did.

The rush of screams all cut short.

Something killed everyone above. At least it sounded that way. The question was…had whatever killed them stopped? Was it over?

We were stranded in the dark basement with a man I gave a bag of potato chips to.

I wondered if he had some keen foresight to take us to a basement or if it was just a rush decision to get us somewhere safe and away from panicking people.

It was warm and muggy in the basement, the melting snow added moisture to the air.

"Thank you," I told the homeless man. "Thank you for saving me. I'm Allie."

"Duane," he told me then looked at my mother.

She didn't say anything.

"This is my mom. Her name is Connie and she thanks you, too," I said. "What made you do it? Was it because I gave you chips?"

"What?" he asked confused. "That was you?"

I nodded.

"Um, no. You two were the only ones still in the car. And you looked young. My daughter's age. I guess fifteen."

"Where is she now?" I asked.

"She's in Seattle with her mom. Hopefully Seattle is safe from this."

"Can we..." My mother waved out her hands. "Stop. Okay. Casual conversation doesn't have a place here right now. We are forty miles from home, and we need to get there."

"Ma'am, I don't know if it's safe to go out," Duane said.

"Mom, there's supposed to be radiation."

"And, honestly, Allie, what difference it that small bit of floor above us going to make? If there's radiation up there, it's down here, too."

"Can we at least wait?" I asked. "Please, just wait a couple hours and then we'll go."

"If there's high levels of radiation—"

"Mom."

"Fine, we'll wait."

I know what had to be going through her mind as we waited out the clock.

Each hour we tried to protect ourselves was another hour we wouldn't make it home, another hour that Dad, Josh and Sean would be exposed.

I hoped they stayed in the bathroom.

She gave us three hours. That was it. Although without a phone it was hard to tell what time it was. Good thing Duane had a watch. My mother was quiet. I knew she was worried, how could she not be?

I was worried.

But she seemed so focused on getting home that she forgot it was forty miles away. We weren't walking that in a couple of hours.

Unless we found a means of transportation, we would have to stop for the night.

The wishful thinking part of me felt like everything was fine. That we would go up top and people would be wandering around, looking for answers just like us.

My mother was anxious, following the blue of Duane's wind-up light as he walked to the door.

Maybe it wasn't the right time to be slightly angry with her. But she didn't seem to care about anything but getting out of that basement. Wasn't she scared? If not, why wasn't she concerned if I was or not?

I held on to my things, clutching them close to me.

Duane looked apprehensive as he stood by the door. Nervously, he pushed the old dresser out of the way and it popped open some.

When he opened the door, the sun blasted through. It wasn't any brighter than when we went in, actually it was probably less bright. But the heat was intense.

It felt like a scorching day in July instead of January.

The truck was still blocking the door and we squeezed beyond it.

The heat was intense, I could see it rippling off the ground when I stepped away from the truck, otherwise everything looked the same.

Except the smell, there was a weird smell.

It reminded me of when my mom's car was doing that overheating thing.

There weren't any sounds. No cars or people. We were in the back of the building and I attributed the lack of noise to that.

Duane moved slowly. I walked along side of him. My mother, in her impatience, picked up the pace and walked ahead of us.

"Everything is fine," she said. "We're not getting home at this pace."

"Connie," Duane called her. "We don't know what happened."

"We'll find out now, won't we?"

It was like my mother was angry about this event that happened, as if there was a way to control it and someone screwed up.

When Duane pulled me from the car and rushed us down to the basement, everything was a blur. As we headed back toward the road, I realized the overgrown hillside was indeed a driveway and it surprised me that no one else followed us.

I suppose they just wanted to find shelter.

We walked toward the main road and the smell grew strong. The cars were still in the road, at first view they didn't look damaged, then I saw the paint had rippled and some were even scorched.

Neither the thrift store nor the other building looked destroyed. They were normal, some black marks on them, but that was it. It was when we reached the street that it became clear.

Dropping his bags, Duane grunted out, "oh my god."

At first I was like, "What? What? What do you see?"

My mother stepped forward, brave faced, unfazed. She looked left to right then up to the sky.

I didn't understand at first, what had they seen?

Again, everything looked normal until my foot hit into something.

It was a purse. One of those hard, square large brown things. The type older women carried. It was on the ground. But it wasn't the purse, it was the black ash. Not in a pile but in the perfect shape of a human body.

One ash arm on the purse, the other reaching out, legs twisted.

After seeing her, I saw others. Some were piles, as if dropped where they stood, some were piles that looked similar to a human form, and the worst were the ones that seemed to have been burned so quicky they were nothing but shadows on cars.

I watched my mother turn and walked toward the store.

"Mom, what are you doing?"

"I have to see."

"See what? Are you crazy?"

She kept moving.

"Mom!"

Picking up her pace, she walked to the front. The windows were intact except for the ones presumably broken in the mad rush to get in.

I didn't want to go inside the store, I didn't. It scared me. Why would she want to see what happened to those people whose screams were cut short?

Despite what I wanted to do, I went inside.

The sour burnt smell was horrendous and overwhelming.

She kept walking toward the back looking around.

I was scared I'd step on remains. Piles of thick black ashes were scattered everywhere just like outside.

But the farther I followed my mother inside, the less incinerated the bodies became.

The more they were protected from the sun, the more of their bodies remained.

Charred, still smoldering.

"Mom, can we go?" I asked shakily. "Please."

My mother finally stopped walking.

"Mom?"

"Oh my God," she turned some, looking over her shoulder at me. "Some of these people are still alive."

NINE

THE INVISIBLE ELSE

It didn't take long.

My stomach twisted and hurt, then it formed a lump that traveled up my chest and made my mouth fill with spit. It came fast like a fountain in my mouth. The next thing I knew I was racing out the door to vomit. I couldn't control it. It just erupted from me.

I never thought something would cause me to instantly throw up.

Those poor people did.

Twisted in a mound, their flesh charred so badly that some parts the bones were exposed.

Their eyes were white with no eyelids, no blinking. No lips, just teeth. Mouths opening and closing, calling out silently in pain. They were meshed and melted together.

The smell was horrendous, but it was nothing compared to the fact that they were still alive.

They wouldn't be for long. How much pain were they in, how sickening it was: I couldn't stand it.

I vomited and then I cried.

Immediately I thought of my brothers and father. Would they be like the people in the thrift store?

Thinking of that made me sick again. What was happening? My body trembled out of control as I stood outside that store.

"Hey," Duane came out. "Are you alright?"

"No. No," I wept. "I didn't want to see that. I don't want to see any of this."

"I know."

"Where's my mother?"

Duane pointed back. "She's still in there."

"How?" I said, breathless. "How can she stay in there? I want to go home."

"Your mom said it's forty miles away. It's a long walk."

"What about the cars that weren't running when this thing hit?" I asked. "Do you think they'll work?"

"I don't know."

"We have to try."

"We will. I…" his word trailed off as my mother walked slowly from the store.

"Allie." My mother walked to me. "Come here."

She reached to me and I fell into her arms. "How could you stay in there?"

"I didn't want to leave them," she said. "They're still alive Allie. Alone, in pain and alive."

"I want to go home. I want to find Dad, Sean, Josh. I'm scared."

"Me, too. But it's a long walk."

"We have to try cars that weren't running," I told her. "Maybe they'll start."

"We can do that," my mother spoke calmly.

Duane looked up. "Sun is bright. It has to be near ninety. We're gonna need water."

"I have-" I fumbled with my bag that hung on my shoulder. "I have a couple bottles in here."

"I have some, too," Duane said. "Down in the basement where we were. I'll grab them. We'll need all we can."

I nodded. "Okay."

"Thank you," My mother told him.

"I'll be right back." Duane turned and hurried back down that overgrown driveway.

My mother watched him until he disappeared from our sight, then she grabbed my arm. "Let's go."

"What?"

"Now, Allie. Move fast. We have to run." She pulled my arm.

"He went to get water."

"Exactly and we have a chance to go."

"Mom."

"Allie, move!" She tugged harder.

"We can't leave him behind."

"And we can't have him with us."

"He saved our lives."

"I don't care. I appreciate it but don't care about him. I care about you. We don't know him. I am not going to trust a stranger."

I pulled away from her. "I'm not going to leave him. I'm not. That's not right. He saved our lives."

"What is the matter with you?"

"Me?" I asked.

"Yes, Allie, you. He was on his own before us. We don't even know that he wants to come with us. Now…move."

It was my mother. She had that hold on me no matter how wrong I thought she was. I huffed, folded my arms and made one more defiant stance as I turned my body from her.

My eyes shifted to the window of the Thrift Store, and I saw them.

Bikes. People had donated them and of course they were there unsold. It was winter.

"Mom, I know how we can get home without walking."

"How?"

Slowly, I walked back toward the store. The front left window was like one of those old-fashioned department store windows. Two bikes along with a wagon were on display there.

We stared at them, knowing that they were our only transportation solution. At least until we found a working car. I saw Duane's reflection in the window and I turned around.

"Hey" he said. "Whew! I thought you guys left me. I didn't see you."

I shifted my eyes to my mother.

"I wanted to leave you," my mother told him. "Allie wouldn't. Or we'd be long gone."

Wow. Talk about being brutally honest.

Duane looked shocked. "I'm sorry. I'll stay back." He lifted a duffel bag that looked packed. "Let me give you some of the stuff. I have a ton. You know, to keep you going."

"My mother wanted to leave you," I said. "Because she thought we were forcing you to come with us."

"Don't lie to the man, Allie. Just don't," my mother said. "And Duane, I apologize. I was just scared. And I wasn't sure you wanted to come with us."

"I just assumed," Duane replied. "You know with everything happening. I thought you'd want me along."

"We do," I said. "I do. Will you come with us? I know you're probably worried about your family and want to find them."

"They're in Seattle. I don't need to go with you. I'll…I'll stay back."

"No." My mother shook her head. "I was wrong. Please come with us. Safety in numbers. Right?"

Duane looked a bit apprehensive about answering that question. He nodded. I moved the conversation away from the awkwardness to the bikes in the window. There were only two there and of course, they had been destroyed. The metal was burnt and the tires melted. But of course, Duane knew where there were more in the store. Down below in his little basement hideaway.

I didn't worry about him or see a problem. My mother's sudden switch in demeanor confused me. I couldn't worry about that. We were all scared. That had to be what it was.

At least we wouldn't be walking in the heat. We had a means to travel. It was time to go.

TEN

LONG STRETCH

The bikes didn't take us far. At least not riding them. As soon as we pulled them from the store, we knew we weren't going to be able to ride them. The tires needed air. Duane suggested a gas station not far up the road. About another mile.

It was still late afternoon. Enough daylight was left to make it worth going as far as we could and getting as close to home as possible.

That was if the sun even set.

The strange fear of that idea hit me as we walked the bikes up the four-lane road. What if the sun didn't even set and just baked us to death while the other side of the world was cast into complete cold and darkness?

It felt it. The temperature was so hot. I wondered if it was because we had been in super cold weather or because it was just that hot.

I knew it wasn't a long walk to the gas station, but it was long enough to think about everything.

The road was wet from the instantly melted snow. I could tell it had been a lot more wet at some point. It had just evaporated from the heat.

We moved along, pushing our bikes through the cars and trucks on the road. Vehicles, like ours, that had just died. I tried not to look at remains. I wondered if a lot of people ran for cover and how many weren't spared because they were exposed to the killer sunlight.

My mother led the way as if she knew exactly where we were going. She probably did. It was a road she took a lot so she was probably aware of the gas station.

She was angry about Duane coming along. I didn't get it. How easily she forgot that he was the reason that we continued to live.

Duane walked along side me.

"Why didn't some things burn?" I asked my thoughts out loud. "The people did. Some of the paint on the cars. But that lady's purse, it was fine."

"I don't know," Duane replied. "Maybe it's the make up of whatever burned. It was ultraviolet rays, I'm guessing, right?"

"Some super strong ultraviolet rays," I said.

My mother huffed slightly. "You realize the sun went nuts. It just blasted us. None of us are scientists so we can only guess. Keep walking."

Duane shifted his eyes to me as if to say, 'what is wrong with your mom?'

I paused to take a sip of my water; it was warm, too warm. I brought some into my mouth and let it rest in there. I didn't want to drink too much too fast.

"You hungry?" he asked.

"Yeah, I am. I have stuff in my bag." I reached for my backpack.

"No, don't. Here." He extended something to me. It was in this odd blue wrapper. The white lettering said 'granola bar', no company name.

"I never saw this brand."

"They come in these things called Blessing Bags, some church passes them out. Everything is in plain blue wrapping like that. Chips, cookies, peanut butter, entrée. Ever see an MRE?"

"MRE?" I asked.

"Meals Ready to Eat, it's what soldiers get."

"Oh, oh, yeah, I have. In movies," I replied.

"Same thing. Only blue wrappers. Turn it over."

I did and chuckled. "The church name and number."

"In case you want to call them."

"I don't want to take your food," I told him.

"No, it's fine. I have a lot." He lifted his head and turned it toward my mother. "Connie, did you want a bar?"

"No. I would like for you two to move a little."

It was then that I realized, in our brief exchange about the generically wrapped granola bar, we had stopped walking.

I thanked Duane again for the bar and unwrapped it, placing the wrapper in my back pocket as if littering really mattered at that moment.

It was good, I was hungry, and I nibbled on that bar as we walked.

<><><><>

My mother nearly kicked the air pump at the Sun Rise Gas Station and Convenience store. She slammed the little handle, and instead of hooking on to the machine, it dangled, the hose to the ground. "Electric," she said. "Great. Just great. No air, no inflating the flat tires."

"There should be one in the store," Duane stated. "Probably in the backroom. Hopefully, the sun blast didn't hit it."

"How do you know?" I asked.

"I worked at a convenience store. They have them on hand in case of power outages," Duane replied. "I'll go look. Maybe we should get supplies. For your family. If there are any in there. Take what we can."

"No," my mother replied quietly. "We move on. We'll find something somewhere else."

"Mom, I don't understand. We just go in and…" I turned around to point at the store and saw what she had.

A man stumbled out. Staggering left to right, like some sort of zombie. He stopped and teetered. The left side of his face was burned and blistered, as well as his clothes.

"Can you help me?" he asked. "I can't see very well. If someone is there, can you help me?"

Without hesitation my mother blurted out, "No."

"Mom?" I looked at her with question and some embarrassment. I mean, did she seriously just say 'no' to helping someone?

49

"We help no one, Allie," My mother replied. "We have to go home."

"But Mom—"

"How do you suppose we help him?" she snapped. "Huh? Can you help him?"

"No."

"Duane, can you help him?" she asked.

"No, ma'am," Duane replied. "But—"

"Then let's go."

I looked down to my water bottle and walked over to the man, ignoring my mother's call of my name.

"Duane," I said. "Find the pump."

"Allie?" My mother called me. "What are you doing? Now is not the time to be defiant."

"I'm not being defiant, just trying to be humane."

"Now is not the time for that either."

"Seriously?" Shaking my head, I walked toward the man.

Duane spoke softly, pausing as he walked by me. "She's just worried about your family. I'll get the pump." He went into the store.

"I heard you," the injured man said. "Can you help me?"

"I can't," I replied. "I wish I could but I can't. We don't have medical supplies. I don't think there's any help out there. There really isn't. There's nobody." I placed my water bottle in his hands. 'This is what I can give. Can I help you back inside where it might be cooler?"

"I just…" he began to weep. "I just wanna go home to my wife and kids. I just wanna go home."

"Got it," Duane announced coming out of the store. He lifted a box with a handle, somehow I expected a bicycle pump.

"Give that to my mom," I instructed. "Then will you help me get him inside and comfortable?"

"Yes, sure." Duane held the pump and walked by me.

"I just wanna go home," the man repeated. "If you see my wife, tell her I wanted to come home."

"I will. Just tell me her name once we get inside."

It was so hot already and I could only imagine how badly it hurt his wounds. I tried not to look at them. They emitted a strong odor.

My mother watched me disapprovingly. I hoped Duane was right that it was just worry and not some secret personality of her's that emerged under crisis.

Duane helped me get the man inside. We found a spot in the back by the coolers. We helped him to the floor, allowing his back to rest against the metal of the milk cases. He told me his wife's name was Janice. I would never meet her, I knew that. But if it gave him comfort to think I would, there was nothing wrong with it.

The man was dying and Duane said he had to be delirious with pain.

There was nothing else we could do but make him comfortable, give him water and leave him to die.

It was horrible. I hated it.

My sixteen-year-old enthusiasm was gone. I never thought anything as bad as this would happen.

But it did.

If my mother's suddenly selfish outlook on humanity was any indication of what the world would become, I was going to hate it.

I always felt so mature, yet at that moment, I felt young. Too young to be facing it. I just didn't see how we could do it. Walk away from every person that needed help.

Then again, if we stopped, would we ever get back home?

ELEVEN

REST UP

I didn't expect the darkness, but it came and it was a relief. A break from the heat, the beating ultraviolet rays that wanted to burn every fiber of my being. It reminded me of one time when we went to the pool and I was confident that I would get a suntan. Instead, I burned. That feeling of burned skin, shivering at night when the temperature didn't warrant it.

The feeling of being cold was welcoming. I knew it was still too hot out.

Somewhere around a place called Large, PA, nearly half-way home, we had to stop for the night.

I thought riding a bike would be easier. That we'd make so much progress. That wasn't the case. We had to stop frequently, drink water, take a break. Rationing the water was the only way. We didn't have much and we weren't sure what the next day would bring.

As we decided we would stop, we saw the camp ahead. Fires created a guiding light. It was set up at the Large Volunteer Fire department just beyond the interchange of Route 51 and Interstate 43.

My mother didn't want to stop. Of course, not. She wanted to move a little past them and halt there. Find a place to stay, at least for a few hours until it was light enough to move on.

At first, I was in agreement.

Then I realized that people had survived. It wasn't just us. Some had found shelter from the blasting sun's rays. However, they weren't completely protected. Unless they were in a basement or shielded from the sun, they had injuries.

The camp was to bring people together, to help them. I wasn't sure who started it or ran it.

It was for those lost, confused and hurt. At least that was what I thought.

It wasn't for us and we didn't need to be there, until the one man approached us.

He looked worn out, like he had worked some sort of long shift. His face was dirty and sweaty and he had this gadget in his hand.

"Let's check you out so we can get you what you need," he said.

My mother abruptly stated, "We aren't staying. We're pushing through."

"Oh, okay, I was just checking you for exposure."

"Exposure to what?" my mother asked.

He looked at the three of us with surprise, as if we should have known. "Radiation," he said.

"We weren't out in it when the thing hit," I said.

"Obviously." He gave a sad smile. "You've been out since, right?"

Duane replied, "We stayed inside for a few hours afterward."

"Well, that's good."

"Wait." I lifted my hand. "Are we still at risk?"

Then my mother said my name as if I were ridiculous. "Allie, enough. Let's go."

"How do you check us?" I asked.

"There's no way to check your blood levels or anything," the man replied. "I can check to see if your clothes are contaminated. If they are then more than likely, you've been exposed."

"Allie, let's go," my mother ordered.

"Mom, don't you want to—"

"No, I don't. If we are, there's nothing we can do about it."

"Not true," the man said. "We have pills that reduce the effects of radiation."

Snidely, my mother faced him. "And how do you have those?"

"I'm a firefighter. We have them in the station in case of nuclear attack."

I asked, "Would it hurt if I took one anyhow?"

"No." The man shook his head.

"Can I have one of these pills?"

Before the man could answer, my mother did. "You are a minor. You are my child. You will not take a pill from a random stranger. Now, move it. Thank you, sir, good luck with everything." My mother began pushing forward.

I looked back at Duane.

"Well, I'm not her child. You can check me and I'll take that pill," Duane said.

I went back and forth from looking at my mother who was now ahead of me and to Duane. I had to catch up to my mother. I told Duane I would see him when he caught up. He understood.

Not able to watch and see if Duane was exposed or contaminated, I hurried to my mother.

There was a good stretch of road until we had passed the area of that camp. I wished we hadn't left. I wanted to know more. Maybe that firefighter had answers. He had lived, survived and wasn't burnt. It also felt safe there. Even though it was all strangers. They were strangers whose stories we could piece together to make sense of everything.

There were a lot of people there and that surprised me. Many were not burnt, but they looked lost. Glancing up to us as we walked by as if we had answers.

And there was a smell that I just couldn't place. Plastic meets metal in a bonfire sort of thing.

My mother was quiet again and I tried, I tried so hard not to be mad at her. Reasoning within myself about why she was acting the way she did.

Cold, abrasive, uncaring. They were the nicer terms that came to mind.

Here we were in some sort of apocalyptic event and I was angry with my mother.

Although I wasn't sure what I had expected, it certainly wasn't to be caught in the aftermath with her. If things were to go nuts, I really thought I would have been at the apartment. Hiding in the bathroom with Josh and Sean.

No sun would get into the windowless room. But would we be exposed? I tried not to think about my father and brothers too much. I was painful to even remotely consider that things could have turned tragic for them.

My father, like my mother, didn't take the storm as seriously.

He too thought I was ridiculous and overreacting when I packed my survival bag.

Maybe that was what weighed heavy on her mind, creating such a foul mood.

Duane was never far behind, although it took him longer than I thought. It just seemed to irritate my mother that he was tagging along. It was hard to explain to Duane that she wasn't being herself and he wasn't to take it personally. Not that it mattered.

He tried to get on her good side, he even offered her the bag the firefighter had given him. A small backpack with water, protein bars, medicine and stuff.

She snubbed it.

I took it. I already was carrying one bag, what was another?

We took refuge in a small lab that did bloodwork for people. Outside, Duane lit a small fire to heat up some soup.

It was too hot of a night to eat anything, but he was nice enough to cook, so I ate it.

My mother wouldn't eat, I tried to give her something.

"I don't want you sitting with him tonight," she said. "Not alone."

"I don't understand."

"Allie, we don't know him. You're a beautiful young girl, you don't know what he is capable of."

"Mom, he saved our lives. We would have been those people on the street."

"I know. I'm grateful."

"Are you?"

"Allie," she snapped my name.

"I'm not asking you to trust him. We should sit together," I told her. "Talk to him. Find out about him. Ever since we left his basement, you've been annoyed that he's with us. That's not fair. Not when he saved us."

"Why us?" she asked. "All those other people he picked us."

"I don't know. Does it matter? We're alive. Talk to him. He spoke to that firefighter, let's find out what he knows. Mom, this isn't you. Okay. I know it's not you. You're not this mean."

"I have to be because I have to protect you. You may be all I have left."

So that was it? As I thought.

I was fine, she could see that, but she had no idea if my father or brothers were and that was where her mind was that.

"Mom, you know, being mean isn't going to change the outcome. We have no idea what happened, let's see if Duane found anything out."

"You can ask him," she flung out her hand.

"He won't tell me without your permission."

She lifted her eyes to me.

"And besides, you said you don't want me alone with him. Come on." I held out my hand. "Let's talk to him."

After a few seconds of being reluctant, she grabbed my hand and stood.

I will say if there was one thing my mother got right, it was staying indoors.

The second we stepped back outside to join Duane the heat was breathtaking, almost too hot to breathe. It was night, why was it getting hotter and did that mean the next day when they sun rose it was going to be even worse?

It wasn't even a day ago when we were buried in snow. "What do you have there?" My mother asked as she sat down by Duane. She referenced the five-gallon paint bucket.

He lifted the lid and looked inside. "It was out back. I think it was there for the winter, filled with water. Probably frozen this morning. I wouldn't drink it. I'm just seeing if keeping it by the fire will make enough condensation to collect water. But it won't be much."

I questioned why.

"Because everything is going to evaporate and we need to find a way to preserve what we can,"

"I don't understand," I said.

"This heat is going nowhere," he replied. "There's no power for pump stations to keep things filtered, so you can't drink the water unless it was in a bottle or your water heater. Those plastic bottles will melt. I don't mean to scare you, but things are bad and they're going to get worse. The water in the rivers, lakes, the reserve at the water plant, all that will go. I mean, there's a way to make the reserves last, but people would seriously have to conserve. Without water, we die."

"Is this what the fire fighter told you?" My mother asked.

Duane shook his head. "No, he told me they were preparing for the worst and the worst happened. He and others made it below before it hit. Actually, they put that warning out."

"We never heard it," my mother said.

I suggested, "Maybe it was when we were in the tunnel."

"Probably," My mother replied.

Duane continued, "It's worse than I thought. The firefighter talked about radiation bursts. Gamma rays, we may or may not have been exposed. The only thing you can do is take potassium iodide"

"Is that what he gave you?" my mother asked.

"Yes."

"Give my daughter what she needs."

"I will do that." He gave a single nod. "I appreciate you doing that and talking to me. I know things have been hard thinking about your husband and sons."

60

"They have, tell me more about this heat wave," my mother said.

Duane chuckled softly. "That's an understatement. It's going to get bad and it won't stop. Once you find your family you're going to need to head to a freshwater area. Not man made. That's what I'm doing. Look at maps, keep going north, staying close to rivers and lakes. Hopefully get far enough north by the time this land is a desert."

"Are you serious?" I asked. "Like we'll turn into Mars?"

Duane looked at me. "That's a great analogy. Allie, it will be unbearable. I would look for temperatures to be over a hundred and humid as the rivers dry up. Severe windstorms, electrical storms. Storms that want to produce rain but won't. Eventually, it will turn. What goes up, comes down. Earth will eventually correct itself, but it will go complete opposite from hot to cold. What you must do as a survivor is find your middle ground."

"You seem very knowledgeable," My mother said. "Was this a job or passion?"

"Both. I was a college professor, earth science, at the community college." He glanced at me. "This was at a time when most people went to a classroom, then it went cyber and there were no jobs."

"You have one now," I told him. 'It doesn't pay much, but you can teach us."

"I'm going to try. If I were to give you one piece of advice it would be take your family and stay away from people as best as you can. For a while."

"Can I ask a question?" my mom lifted her hand. "That bucket is full, how are you planning on bringing that tomorrow?"

"I'm not. It's for us to wet down before we leave," he replied.

"Won't it evaporate on us in the heat?" I questioned. "I would think the sun would dry us right up."

"Yep. It will," he said. "That's why I think we should leave and travel at night. It may not seem it, but it's cooler, our clothes will stay wet longer. The moon is super bright. And by day, we find a basement something to rest."

"You think we should go now?" Mom asked.

"I do. I know I said earlier we needed to stop, but we need to travel when radiation is lowest and the weather isn't at its hottest."

"Then let's go. Allie, get your things." She faced Duane as she stood. "Do they know exactly what it was? I know they said solar storm. But did the firefighter know?"

Duane shrugged. "No one knows. Common sense tells us it was more than a solar storm, it could be a lot of things. But it left us as nothing more..." he said. "Than a scorched earth."

TWELVE

NIGHT VISION

I didn't think it was possible for the night sky to be as bright as it was. Knowing from fifth grade science that the sun was what brightened the moon, I worried.

It was like a white spotlight, a slight halo surrounded it from the heat.

We had at least twenty miles to go. At a steady pace, we could be home by morning.

Before we left, Duane pulled out a hunting knife and cut the legs of my jeans into shorts. I stayed behind the counter of the blood lab while he did so. I had a tee shirt under my sweater, so that was easy.

The knife was big with a wooden handle that had a deer on it.

My mother eyed that knife, possibly with worry.

Duane explained his father had given it to him.

I knew I'd feel better with clothes that weren't so heavy. We left on a winter morning and in the course of twelve hours it had turned into a scorching summer.

My mother wouldn't cut her pants, she said she was fine. I don't know how, it was so hot. I wasn't looking forward to the next day when the sun was at its brightest.

Duane had a map, he pointed out the creeks that my family should follow.

Stay in the woods, in the water.

It didn't take long before we left. I took a dose of that medication, Duane did as well. My mother refused.

Like wearing the winter clothes, she was fine. Maybe she had some weird logic about it. My grandmother did. Always saying that if she had layers of clothes to take off she would feel cooler.

Not me.

That bucket had smelly water, but it felt good. Because the sun wasn't beating down on us, my clothes and hair didn't dry instantly. It really did help keep me cool.

It was hard to tell how far we actually went. Our pace was slow. The air was too thick to chance getting winded. We biked on the road, concrete that had spent the day absorbing the heat, it now radiated it.

My legs started burning. I needed to take a break. The heat was getting to me and my stomach started feeling upset.

"Can we stop?" I asked. "Just for a few minutes. I feel sick."

"When's the last time you drank water?" Duane asked.

"I don't know."

"We'll stop. You need to get hydrated," he said. "Connie, we're stopping."

My mother was ahead of us by ten feet. We didn't have to tell her twice. Immediately, she pulled over and hoped off before the bike had even stopped.

It toppled over, catching her right leg and before she made it a few feet from the bike, she vomited.

It erupted from her. I didn't think anyone could have that much liquid in them.

"Mom!" I jumped off my bike and raced over. "Mommy, you okay?"

She heaven again, forcing more from her gut.

"Connie, did you drink something you shouldn't have?" asked Duane. "Like maybe a juice, anything?"

She shook her head. "Just water. Not much."

I wanted to say that by looking at how much come from her, she could have fooled me.

"Are you sure, Mom?" I questioned. "Absolutely sure, there's a lot coming from you."

"Not since this morning. I drank all that orange juice re-member, but that's it. Sips of water here and there," she an-swered before starting to gag again.

Duane reached over, touching her face, then he grabbed her wrist.

"What are you doing?" I asked.

"Her skin is hot, her heart rate is fast, she is suffering from hyperthermia. We need to bring her core temperature down."

"I'm fine," my mother said.

"No, you're not. Sit," Duane ordered. "Allie, take every-thing we have as far as water goes, make her drink and wipe her down. Take our supplies out of my bag. I have to find water."

"I'm fine." My mother's balance teetered as Duane walked away.

I reached for her, trying to help her. I took her bag from her back and lessened her load.

Aiding my mother in sitting, I checked her bag for her water.

She had several full bottles, which surprised me. Seven of them. "Mom?" I questioned. "Why do you have all this water?"

"We need it."

"Where did you get it from?" I asked. "I only had two. I gave you one."

She turned her body and heaved, futilely fighting back her retching.

"Hey," Duane returned, slightly out of breath.

I looked up suddenly. Pulling my views from my mother's stocked bag,

"Across the street on that Arby's is a hose," he said. "Water is still coming out. We can't drink it, but she can wet her down. Connie, are you sure you didn't drink any water you shouldn't have?"

My mother didn't answer.

"Let me grab a bottle from my stash, Allie, you give it to her make her drink it."

"Okay."

Duane walked over to his bike. Unlike me and my mother, he didn't wear his bag. His was strapped on the back of his bike. He unzipped it and his enthusiasm paused.

"What is it?" I asked.

He shook his head. "I swore I brough more waters. I only have a few." He pulled one out of his bag and extended it to me. "Here."

"No," I said. "We won't take yours."

"Please. I have two more."

I took the water bottle. Then waited until he went back across the street and returned it to his bag.

I returned to my mother and grabbed a bottle from her bag, uncapping it. "Did you take his water?"

"Allie...I'm sick."

"Mom, did you take his water from his bag? Is this his?"

She grabbed the bottle from my hand. "I didn't take his water."

"Then where did you get it from? You didn't..."

"Allie, go away and let me be sick in peace."

I slowly stood from my crouching position, backing up. What was up with her.

She flipped flopped constantly about Duane.

At first she wanted to leave him behind, then she said for him to come, but was nasty and mean to him.

She had to be dealing with stuff I didn't understand.

I left her there to be alone, sitting on the road leaning on her fallen bike.

Duane returned.

He had these white towels, at least they looked white, and he carried them to my mother. He wrapped one over her shoulders and the other over her head. They talked for a second, I couldn't hear what was being said. He nodded, she nodded and then he came over to me.

"I think she'll be okay," he said.

"You don't think it's that radiation stuff, do you?" I asked.

"No, but I can't be sure. I'm fine. How about you?"

"I was a little sick."

"How about now?" he asked.

"Still queasy."

"Drink some water, see how you are after a rest."

"Okay." I sought out my bag and bottle of water. I had another in my bag, but it was mine. I didn't take it from anyone. I felt guilty when I looked at Duane. I was certain my mother took his water, where did she get it from if she didn't?

I sat down on the road. It was warm, nothing was cool at all.

"We'll give it a little and head out again," Duane told me as he joined me. "We're really not that far. A couple more hours maybe."

"Good. And uh, Duane, I'm sorry about my mother."

"Allie, she's sick, she can't help it."

"No, I'm sorry about how she is." I sipped my water. "Some girls have a good relationship with their mother. Friends. I never had that. Ever. She was always untouchable to me. She didn't seem like the other mothers. Like, I don't know, I can't find the word."

"An anomaly," Duane said. "Something that deviates from the norm."

"Maybe." I shrugged. "I just know she wasn't like other mothers. Isn't like them."

"How about your father?"

"He's there in the mystery department as well. It's not that I didn't try. They were always working, traveling for their jobs. When they were home it was cold. My brothers and I are close. It wasn't until we turned poor until they had to be in the same space with us all the time."

Duane chuckled. "Turned poor?"

"Oh, yeah, we had a big house, cars, my mom and dad both had like executive positions. My father was in sales and my mom was, I think it was called Chief Financial Officer of some German pharmaceutical company in Washington. They both worked there."

"You don't know your mom's company?"

"I do, they bounced around a couple times..."

"German Pharmaceutical company. Was it Norvo?" he asked.

"Yeah, it was."

Duane nodded. "So your parents lost everything."

"Yep," I replied. "When my brother got sick my mother had to quit, my father too. He started delivering food. They did what they could. But you know, quitting, they lost the insurance. I didn't understand that. Why quit if your kid has cancer?"

"What did they say about that?" Duane asked.

"That state benefits were better."

Duane lifted his water bottle to his mouth and took a sip as he nodded.

"Anyhow, medical bills were high, they sold everything. The house, cars, everything. We had to move and I don't think she ever got over it."

"How's your brother now?"

"Sick." I sighed out. "We had to go to Pittsburgh for his medicine. That's why we weren't home. I know that's on my mom's mind. Sean needs his medicine."

"Understandable," he said. "It's also hard going from having everything you need to scraping by. Trust me, I know."

"I bet you do."

"Did your brother get sick before or after everything went down with Norvo?"

"What do you mean?"

"Norvo, the company. When it—"

My mother abruptly cut him off when she approached. "It's time to go. We need to move. I need to get home."

"Sure." Duane stood. "Allie, are you alright to go?"

"She's fine," my mother answered.

"I am." I stood and looked at my mom. "Do you have enough water?"

Without responding to that, she turned and walked to her bike in a huff.

"I guess she's feeling better," Duane said.

I muttered out a 'yeah.' I was feeling better myself and wanted to get going.

Like my mother, I just wanted to get home.

THIRTEEN

HOME

The straight shot home was Route 51, but it wasn't the best way in the heat.

We were headed south from Pittsburgh, the opposite direction of the way we needed to go.

Three miles from Uniontown, four miles from my home, we met a man who was digging a hole. It was freaky at first, I thought maybe he was burying someone, but he said it was for him to sleep in.

We spoke to him briefly. He asked if we had any food, just something until he could scavenge a meal that hadn't been scorched.

Duane gave him one of those protein bars.

My mother hated to stop, but I needed to know how and why that man survived.

I asked him. It was like pausing in a video game and some random stranger in the game gives you information.

"They gave a warning," he explained. "Just before the event, anyone watching the news or online knew the worse case scenario, which is not what we're facing. Trust me, by what they said it could have been worse. They said they'd send an alert to get below and if that wasn't possible, then avoid direct sunlight. A windowless room. That's how I survived."

He broke a sweat, pausing in his digging.

"Is it everywhere?" I asked.

"Yes," he nodded. "The other half of the world had warning and time to prepare. More than us." He ran his hand over his brow.

"You realize," Duane said, "You shouldn't be digging in the heat."

"I know, but I think a hole in the ground is better than a basement."

"Did they give any advice?" I questioned. "To survive."

"Dig in and wait it out," he replied. "And that's what I'm doing. They expect a few weeks at most. Unless the storms come early."

Duane asked. "So they aren't advising to go north?"

The stranger shook his head. "It's hot now, by what I gathered, it won't be long before things in the north freeze over. I'm not sure why. And how did you not hear any of this?"

I shook my head. "Not the warnings. We didn't hear."

Duane added. "I only heard because I was running and panicking. I saw her and her mom still in the car and grabbed for them."

"Good luck. Haven't seen many people, then again, they may still be below," he told us.

We thanked him, then appeasing my mother we headed out on the final leg of the walk to our apartment complex.

My mom blurted out a snarky, "Did you get what you needed from him?"

"Yeah, actually, we did," I replied. "You know there's a chance Dad and them got below."

"At the very least, maybe they stayed in the bathroom." My mom hopped on her bike and started to ride.

Duane glanced at me. "The bathroom?"

"There's no window," I explained, getting on my bike. "When I was researching it, online was saying to stay away from the sun. That things will get really bad if the worst happens."

"Allie, why do you keep asking questions if you did research?"

"Because I am hoping I'm wrong."

"I see." He nodded.

"Maybe the basement of the building won't be a bad idea. It is underground and we don't have to stay there long."

"Yeah, what about water? Food? I still think following the stream is the best way to go," Duane said. "Live off nature. To me, staying below is boxing yourself in."

"I don't think my parents or even myself have the skills to survive outside in nature."

"Have you always been so serious and mature?" Duane asked. "I mean, I get you're a teenager, probably close to graduating, but you just seem like a girl who is far too serious."

"Isn't this a serious situation?"

"Of course, it is, but don't you smile?"

I slowed in my peddling, coasting a bit. "I do. I guess lately, before all this even happened, there wasn't much to smile about. Sean is my best friend."

"Sean is your brother?" Duane asked.

"Yeah and he's so sick. I hate it. I don't want to lose him, I don't. It seems everything they did made him worse."

"I'm sorry."

"And now all this. We got his medication, but he'll never get the help he needs. The treatments, the operations, the oxygen. Everything. Everything you take for granted. You know, I get what they mean when they say only the strong survive."

"You can't think like that."

"When you meet my brother, you'll see how awesome he is and why it's so unfair."

"Sounds like life has been unfair for your entire family lately."

"Yeah," I said sadly. "But you haven't had an easy time of it either."

"Guess you're right, life's been a bit unfair to me as well."

My mother suddenly turned her bike and full speed headed back to us, skidding to a stop as if she were trying to intimidate Duane.

"Unfair?" she asked. "You think life was unfair to you? You chose to be homeless."

"Mom!"

"He lost his job, he had a degree, he never found another job. There were plenty out there. It was just easier to pan-handle on the street. No wonder his family is in Seattle."

"Mom!" I scolded again. "You don't know his story."

"And neither do you. Don't." She pointed at me. "Don't raise your voice to me again."

"Let it go," Duane spoke softly. "She doesn't know."

"I know what is unfair," my mother snapped. "And I would label what happened to our family as brutal. Unfair is an understatement."

"I know," he said.

"No, you don't know. You don't know the half of it."

"I think I do," he replied. "I know about Norvo."

On that, she jerked her bike away and sped off.

I looked at Duane. "What do you mean?"

He shook his head and started to peddle again.

We were close, so close. I could see the Rite Aid blocks ahead. It was near our complex and the closer we got, the more scared I felt.

FOURTEEN

BROTHER WHERE ART THO

Our four-building apartment complex was in a residential area, surrounded by small homes.

It never looked like it belonged in the neighborhood. It was more of an out of place eyesore.

I had heard about it before we moved there.

For what it was, the apartments weren't bad. Basic, simple, affordable housing. They were loud at times, cold in the winter.

Flat roof, pink siding under the widows. The name 'Harris Gardens' made it sound fancy and beautiful like resort or something. Why would they do that? Why would they name it something fancy and not call it what it was? Poor People apartments.

Only one of the four buildings actually had a basement, and it wasn't our building.

It looked quiet when we arrived just before daylight. A hint of light in the sky already let me know how hot it was going to be.

From a distance I could see the pink siding on the east facing side of the buildings had been charred.

Some of the windows were blackened out, some broken, some open. I didn't want to look for our apartment, I deliberately avoided it, because I just didn't want to see.

I kept thinking back to the thrift store

All those people out front, outside were incinerated. Those who stayed back but still exposed were burnt.

Those, like us, nowhere near the sun, were fine. At least on the outside.

We had been going all night and I was tired, but a part of me was too anxious to even think about sleep.

What would we find when we walked in?

Would we even find my family? Were they there? Had they escaped? Heard the warning and made it to the basement of Building Four?

I couldn't see my father moving Sean like that. Then again, living was a powerful motivation.

We moved forward. Everything was one step, one breath at a time.

Stepping closer to the building, I could see the charred remains. Bones that were gray and could crumble with any touch, ashy remains surrounding them. Like a barbecue gone wrong. I probably knew some of them, not by name, but in passing.

It made me sad because we hadn't seen a single person alive at all since we left that man with the hole on the side of the road.

I had been fortunate enough to never have to live in a home without air conditioning. Duane wasn't, so when he said, "It feels like using the oven on a hot summer day and opening it," I didn't get the analogy.

He was referring to walking into Building A. Our building.

I could feel the heat as soon as we opened the door.

We lived on that first level, so there were no steps for us to take. I looked over the railing to the stairs and thought of those people who lived below us. Those apartments were half underground. Did they survive?

In silence we walked straight ahead, opening the metal door that led to our apartment. Second door on the right.

The hallway was dark, but untouched by the scorching sun. There were no windows.

My mother led the way and then she stopped as she reached for the handle.

"I can't." her hand hovered the knob. "I can't go in there." She looked at me. "I can't face it if they're gone. What if they're like everyone else?"

"We have to know, Mom," I replied.

"Would you like me to go?" Duane asked.

"Yes, please, thank you," My mother replied.

"No," I stated abruptly. "I'll do it."

"Allie, it's not a good idea," my mother said.

"I'm going to see one way or another." I walked to the door. "What difference does it make if I see it first or last?" I turned the knob, it was locked.

I heard the jingling of keys and my mother handed me her keyring. Her hands shook as she did so.

Her human side had come through. All that anger and bitterness was just a coverup for her fear. A fear I was also feeling at that moment.

It was overwhelming, I had never in my life felt anything like it.

I unlocked the door, but also had to do the deadbolt, which was odd because we never used the deadbolt during the day.

Slowly, apprehensively, my heart beating hard in my chest, I turned the knob and pushed open the door. It wasn't completely dark in the apartment; daylight made its way through.

A lump formed in my throat.

The sun came in.

A few steps down the short hall brought me to the main room, the big one.

The picture window was busted, Sean's bed was blackened, as was the carpet and everything else in the living room.

There were no bodies. At least none I could see.

"What is that noise?" Duane asked.

I listened. It was a slight hissing, steady.

"Sounds like water," Duane stated and turned his head. "This way." He pointed past the kitchen the little hall that led to the bedrooms.

I hurried that way; the sound grew louder. Duane was right. The sound was running water and when I arrived at the bathroom door, I could hear it.

Ear to the door, I couldn't hear voices, only a light spraying sound. Water trickling at a slow rate.

I lifted my eyes to my mother and she nodded.

Before my mother and I left for Pittsburgh, I had moved supplies into the bathroom, certain that after we left my father would move them out.

But had he?

I turned the knob and pushed open the door, scared beyond belief of what I would find.

Immediately a dim orange hue crept out. The small bathroom was lit by a single candle sitting on the sink. Opening the door wider, I saw my family.

My father, Sean and Josh all sat in the bathtub. A slow stream of water trickled on them from the running shower.

The relief I felt escaped me in a form of a gasping scream. My knees buckled and I couldn't move.

I was so grateful.

They were alive.

FIFTEEN

ELSEWHERE

Alive but not well.

That was exactly what I thought when I saw them. My father was pale, Josh hung half over the tub. A trail of vomit went down the side of the tub to the floor. And Sean could barely move.

All that was there were the four empty bottles of water. The same amount I brought in.

Our bathroom which was only as wide as a tub and not much longer than a closet was a smelly, hot box. The air in the was stale and thick. The occasional turning on of the shower that my father did to cool them down only mixed with the heat and made the bathroom tropically humid.

"We need to get them out of here," said Duane.

"But where?" I asked.

"Out of this bathroom. In the hall," he explained. "Then we'll find a place, somewhere other than here. Let's move them and get them water."

My mother whimpered, then released a single sob as she reached for my brother Josh. "Baby, wake up."

I watched Josh open his eyes slightly. I heaved out a breath. Hearing my mother beg for him to wake up had made me fearful that he was gone.

My brother Sean lay with his head against the spicket.

Duane moved into the room and reached for Josh, lifting him out of the tub.

My brother wasn't a big kid, but he was still too tall for Duane and his legs flopped over the tub. "Come on, son," Duane spoke to him. "I need you to stand, can you try for me? Hold on to your mom."

Like a bobble head, Josh nodded.

MY mother wrapped on arm around him.

"Allie, help your mom."

I rushed over to hold up Josh on his other side. I saw what Duane was doing. He extended a hand to my father. More than likely he was trying to get my father out of that tub to help Sean. The three of them were squashed together in there.

My father teetered as he stood, grabbing on to the wall as he tried to climb out with Duane's help.

"This is all dehydration and heat," Duane explained. "One we get them out of here and into that hall with water, it will help."

I knew we had water for them, at least a few bottles. My mother did in her bag. Maybe this was why she stole them. She had a feeling or something. I reasoned with her actions in my mind as I helped her bring Josh out of the bathroom and apartment and into the hallway outside.

Josh felt cool and clammy, his skin was super pale and just as we set him down on that ugly brown hallway carpeting, my father came out. He collapsed next to josh and looked at my mom.

"I'm sorry, Connie, I tried."

"It's fine," my mother replied. "We'll be okay." She opened her bag and pulled out a bottle of water, handing it to my father, then another for Josh.

It's fine? Was that really her response?

Thinking I needed to go help Duane, I turned to go back in the apartment. As I did, Duane emerged with Sean in his arms.

Sean was much taller than Josh, but he weighed so much less. He was mere skin and bones to begin with. His arms draped over Duane's, and he could barely respond.

The moment Duane set him on the floor, it was clear to me that my already dying brother was now on a fast-track course.

"Sean." I crouched down to him. "Sean, look at me."

Sean stared out, barely blinking. I grabbed for my bag; I still had a bottle of water left.

Looking at my family was like a twisted version of Goldie locks and the Three Bears, all levels of strength, none of them very good. Strong chair, soft chair, weak chair. My father, the Papa Bear, was strong enough to drink from his own bottle. Next in the weaker line was Josh he drank with my mother's help, but Sean, he could barely lift his head enough when I brought the water to his lips.

"Please drink," I begged him. "Please." I put some water in the cap and pulled his bottom lip to open his mouth, dumping the water in there.

It dribbled down the side of his lips and his eyes raised to me.

"I know you're sick," I told him. "Please drink for me."

I filled another cap, repeating my actions. It felt so futile.

"I have an idea," Duane said. "We saw that Rite Aid. Maybe somewhere in there is a syringe. I'll go find one. Then look for a place we can all go for the day. Underground, cooler."

"Okay," I said. "I'll go with you." I attempted another cap full and handed my mother the bottle. "Will you try to get him to drink."

"Of course," my mother replied. "Allie, I wish you wouldn't go."

"I want to get what we need. I know the area better than Duane. I'll be back."

My mother gave me a closed mouth smile, a gentle look conveying that it was okay. She still helped Josh drink his water.

I hated, absolutely hated leaving Sean. A part of me felt as if I were abandoning him. He felt separated from my father and Josh, like the runt.

"Sean, I'll be back," I told him.

Sean weakly reached for my hand.

"Hold on. I won't be long." I then stood.

"You sure?" Duane asked me.

"Yeah. Positive." I grabbed my bag and shouldered it.

I was completely exhausted, moving on pure adrenaline and fear. Even as tired as I was, I knew I couldn't rest until I got my family what they needed. Water and a safe place to go.

SIXTEEN

FRAUGHT

Stepping out of the apartment building was another world. It felt completely different than heading home. Before it was a focused journey to get where we needed to go: one track mind, one track destination.

Stay cool, calm, get home.

Now I was home, and everything took on a new meaning.

I had thought the hallway was hot until I stepped outside, the temperature had soared in the short amount of time we had been inside.

I could feel the heat coming from the concrete into my shoes, there was no breeze and I swore I could hear the leaves on the trees sizzle.

It was so unbelievably hot that there was no way we could move fast. Slow motion, molasses steps, darting into shade wherever we could find it.

I know our area well and unlike the journey home, I could see the damage done.

Very few windows on the east side remained. Anything flammable facing the son was burnt. I didn't want to think about how many people had died, I focused on how many people got the warning and hid from the window.

It had zapped the world like an X-ray machine with disintegrating powers.

I wondered how much protection the trees would give everything and with the heat, how long it would last.

"That man," I said to Duane. "The one we met on the edge of town, he said weeks. What do you think?"

"Weeks until it changes? That's what I took him to say," Duane replied. "I think it will be longer. Not much though. I think everything is going to dry out and have to eventually cause storms for things to shift back. That's what I think. But who knows, right?"

"Yeah. But what do we do in the meantime? Is it going to get hotter?"

"I don't know."

"I keep thinking about Mars and how this may have happened to that planet."

"Allie, they never found proof that Mars was really as green as earth," Duane said. "Let alone that it supported a life form such as ours. Man will find a way. We just need to hold out on the water."

"I thought you said there won't be any without power to pump it through. Yet, my dad was running the shower."

"That's probably what remained in the water heaters. Once they're empty it will stop. That's also an option for water of we don't find any. Search out the building's hot water tanks."

"Every apartment has their own," I explained.

"Even better."

Water.

For some reason I kept think about the bottle of water I left for Sean. I don't know why but I worried that my mother was going to focus more on Josh than Sean. I mean, that was where her attention went.

Josh wasn't dying.

Sean was.

At least not before the incident.

I needed to hear from my father about everything that happened in that twenty-four hours. How did they go from thinking I was insane to running to the bathroom for protection?

They had to have heard the warning.

"Do you think my mother will give Sean water?" I asked.

"What?" Duane stopped walking. "Why would you ask that?"

"I just worry."

"Of course, she will, that's her child."

"So why didn't she run to help him first?"

"She went to her baby," Duane replied without skipping a beat. "Don't worry about it, Allie, and even if she doesn't, we'll find water and be back soon. We'll get him water. But..." The Duane just stopped talking.

I thought maybe he saw something, but that wasn't the case.

"But what?" I asked.

"He was very sick beforehand," he said. "You just need to remember that, okay?"

"I do."

"It's very sad. Maybe he'll end up being stronger than us all," Duane said. "I just don't want you to not trust your mother."

Mistrust in my mother? I guess fearing she would withhold water from Sean was in a sense a mistrust.

"I take it you and your mom didn't always see eye to eye?" he asked.

"Not really. We fought, or rather bickered."

Duane nodded. "That's normal for teenage girls to have that with their mom."

"Is your daughter like that with her mom?" I asked. "I know you said she's my age and with her mom in Seattle."

Duane lowered his head. "I have to apologize to you."

"For what?"

"I wasn't totally honest."

I stopped walking for a second and looked at him. Expecting him to tell me he wasn't really a father or something on those lines.

"My daughter is with her mom," Duane said. "Her...her ashes. She passed away last year."

I felt my heart skip a beat. "Oh my God, I am so sorry."

"It's okay. I am too. She was sick. Like Sean. But it was the medication that did it. It was contaminated. That's how I knew about Norvo."

"I don't understand. What happened with Norvo?" I asked. "You said something about it to my mom."

"Let's drop it." He started to walk. "I know that Rite Aid isn't that far."

89

"It's not." I reached out and grabbed his arm. "What happened?"

He inhaled than let out his breath. "It's not my place to tell you if your parents didn't. I could be wrong. Just a lot went down with Norvo. Several people lost their jobs, purged, because of financial missteps. Claiming they embezzled. Now…" he lifted his hand. "It could be entirely possible they were setting people up to divert attention from the contaminated medication. But I am willing to wager, your mom was a casualty of the purge."

My hand remained on his arm, though my grip had loosened.

Instantly I thought back to before she gave up her job for my brother. The arguments between her and my father. Their little whispering arguments. It was about money, always about money and moving. I thought they were selling things to pay for Sean's care. How stupid was I? If my parents had jobs that were that good, why were we selling off things to help Sean?

Duane implied she could have been a pawn in Norvo creating a cover up. Maybe she was. Maybe she wasn't.

Really, other than creating another level of mistrust, what my mother did or didn't do at Norvo no longer matter in the world the way it was.

At least I didn't think so.

As we made it closer to the Rite Aid, I struggled with why I was focused on something so unimportant when everything was going on.

I felt like a horrible person for not trusting my mother, other things were more important.

But was that trust warranted? After all, she did take Duane's water and I kept going back to her helping Josh and ignoring Sean.

For all I knew everything could have been a magnified product of my imagination.

Four blocks.

We made it the four blocks in the intense heat, not that I thought going into a store would make things better.

It would at least be shade from the glaring sun.

As we approached the Rite Aid, I felt defeated. The large pharmacy that had everything from food to toys was missing all the windows. Crossing the parking lot, I could see the front end was much like the Thrift Store, blown out and burned out.

"There's not going to be any water in there," I said.

"You don't know."

"Yeah, I do, look at it." I walked closer.

"There's no windows in the back," he said.

"So?"

"So that's where they keep the storage. We'll go in the back and see." Duane looked determined and unfazed by the condition of the Rite Aid.

Half the sign was gone, it looked as if it were destroyed years before instead of a day ago.

We walked through the broken window onto the charred floor. I didn't want to look to see if there were bodies, I had seen enough.

I followed his lead, the further from the front windows we walked, the less damage there was.

The pharmacy was located in the far back and didn't look like it was too damaged.

"Hold on." Duane climbed over the blackened counter.

"What are you doing?"

I watched him walked toward the shelves.

"Looking for medication. Antibiotics and stuff will be good to have on hand. But…"

"But?"

He stepped back out. "Someone cleared these shelves."

"I see all kinds of pills."

"But the shelf for antibiotics is cleared off."

"So others are alive?"

Duane nodded. "Obviously. And they're thinking ahead like us. Alright, let's go check the back."

He climbed back over the counter and walked around the pharmacy. In the small hall by the restrooms was a solid metal door with a bar handle across the front.

Duane pushed on it and stepped inside.

My hand reached for the door to go through when I heard him.

"Oh, wow, bingo."

As I stepped through, the temperature was slightly cooler, enough to feel the difference.

Around us were bins and pallets of items still wrapped.

"Unbelievable," he said.

Another interjection from him in regards to something he saw that I didn't. He raced across the room.

"What is it?"

"A washing station." He looked over his shoulder and smiled at me.

He then pointed to what looked like a stationary tub. The sink had a green hose that ran to a white plastic container. The spicket was arched with what looked like a shower head.

"What's a washing station?" I asked.

"Exactly what it sounds like. Self-contained, distilled water for washing." At the sink he stepped on a pedal and water squirted from the shower head. Duane caught it and splashed his face. "Feels good."

I moved closer to the sink. "Should we be using that?"

"It's not drinking water. It could be. Just a little won't hurt. Look soap." He reached for it.

"Stop," I told him. "Don't. Look at it."

"What?"

He didn't see what I did. The soap glistened a bit. "Duane, that's wet. Someone was here recently. They might still be."

Just as I said that I heard this sound. A shifting, clicking sound. While I had never heard it in real life, I recognized the sound from movies.

It was a gun and it was close.

"We are," the woman's voice said. "Step away from the sink. Hands in the air."

SEVENTEEN

DISCOVERY

Hand lifted, both Duane and I slowly turned around.

The prospect of having a rifle pointed at me should have scared me more, but somehow it didn't.

The moment I saw the woman and the two young boys just behind her, I knew she wasn't shooting me. Not in front of the kids. Plus, if she was going to shoot me, she would have done so already.

The boys were twins, that much was easy to tell. They couldn't be older than ten. They looked scared, but oddly enough, clean.

The woman was younger than my mother and didn't hold the rifle like someone that knew what they were doing.

"How did you survive?" she asked.

"We were underground," I replied. "In a store basement in Pittsburgh."

"Pittsburgh? That's a ways off."

"Can you..." Duane stammered some. "Can you lower the gun? We don't have weapons. We're not armed. We aren't here for any harm."

"We just need water," I said.

"No, you need to go," she told us. "Leave. Go back to Pittsburgh."

"I'm not from Pittsburgh. I live in the Harris Apartments a few blocks away," I told her. "Can you please put down that gun? I'm just a kid."

Slowly, she lowered it and faced the twins. "Go on, get in the back. I'm good. Go now." The boys ran off and she faced me again. "I need you to go honey. We claimed this place."

My shoulders ached and it felt good to put down my hands. "And that's fine. It's fine. I just need water."

"I'll give you a bottle and then you go."

I shook my head. "I need more. If you have more, I could use it."

"What we have here is for me and my family. I'm sorry. I will tell you one more time to go."

"Come on." Duane took my arm. "We'll find something."

"No." I shook my head and pulled away. "No." I then looked at the woman. "I get it. You survived. You got the warning and were smart enough to come here. This is yours."

"It is," she said. "And I have to make it last. They said it could be weeks before things change. I need everything I can get for my kids."

"And I need something for my family. Look," I stepped to her. "I not gonna beg you because you are not the type of woman that needs to be begged. My brothers are dying. They need water. One is thirteen, the other is seventeen and he was sick before all this. I'm not asking for me, I'm asking for them."

"Where are they?" she asked.

"At the apartment building," I answered.

"You need to get them far away from windows and anything that's too far above ground. Heat rises."

"I don't have a choice," I replied. "They can't go anywhere yet."

"What about your parents?" she asked.

"I'm not asking for them. I'm asking for my brothers."

"And you?" she questioned.

"I'm okay."

"Are you? Because those sores on your arms tell me you've been out there too long. You were out there since it happened."

I was going to respond then it registered what she had said to me.

Sores on my arms?

I wasn't even aware I had any until she said that, then I looked to my left forearm. Sure enough, there were several purple marks that looked like burns. I whimpered when I saw them. I literally froze looking at them.

"Hey, hey," Duane spoke soothingly. "It's okay. You're taking the potassium iodide, it will help."

"No, it won't," said the woman. "It prevents the thyroid from processing it. Obviously, she started taking it too late. She needs Prussian Blue, that removes the radiation poisoning."

"Radiation poisoning?" I asked panicked.

"That's what that is baby girl," she said. "You need that to get you better: rest, that medicine and water. I know what I'm talking about. I'm not a doctor but I am, or was, a pharmacist here."

Duane asked. "Is there any here?"

"Yes. But she can't just take it and be off. She has to be monitored," said the woman. "She needs to stay out of the sun. I'm not sure if the radiation levels are still high but she can't take a chance right now."

My eyes were locked on my sores. I wished I had sleeves just to cover them up. I felt fine.

"Listen." She stepped closer. "You said Harris Apartments, right? Why doesn't this man take the water to your family and you stay here? I'll look after you. He can come back."

"I can't," I whimpered. "My brother Sean may not make it and I don't want to be away from him."

She placed her hand on my face and looked at me. "You're burning up. You need to hydrate and stay in. Okay."

I nodded.

"Find me if there's problems. I'm not going anywhere."

I knew it. I was right about her. She wasn't violent. She was gentle and caring. She didn't want to shoot us or not help us, she just needed to protect her kids and whatever she had to give them.

The woman faced Duane. "In the back you'll see a large pallet of water. Take a case. But that's all I can give you."

"That is enough, thank you," replied Duane.

He was out of my sight all of thirty seconds when I heard him call out.

"Allie, oh my God, Allie, come here."

I saw it in the woman's face, slight fear that maybe he was up to something. She lifted her gun and raced back ahead of me.

Duane just stood there with his back to us. He stood before a desk, probably the managers desk. His eyeline was on the corkboard above the desk.

"What's wrong?" I asked.

"Nothing is wrong." He turned and smiled. "Allie, I know where we can all go."

EIGHTEEN

RITE PLACE

Her name was Ayana Smeed, but she said to just call her Aya. She had worked at the Rite Aid for four years as a pharmacist, but before that worked her way up from cashier, while going to school and doing her internship at the hospital.

She was married and had three sons. The twins, Job and Hamm, and an oldest son near my age named Noah. I wasn't sure, but I was willing to bet she was pretty religious.

Her husband wasn't with her in Rite Aid.

I got all that from her in a couple minutes.

When everyone else ran for cover, she and her boys ran to the back room and hoped for the best. Her husband was working and she hadn't heard from him since.

In fact, we were the first people she had seen since the event.

Her son, Noah, had returned just after Duane made the discovery.

Dressed in layers that were too much for the heat, Noah went looking for his father. He was given two hours. No more.

He was angry when he saw us, but listened to his mother when she told him to pipe down.

"You're giving these people water?" he barked. "How do you know they aren't coming back and taking the rest of our stuff?"

"What would you prefer me to do?" she asked. "Shoot them?"

"Yes."

"Oh, stop."

"Why are we staring at the cork board?" Noah asked.

Aya didn't answer him, she looked at Duane. "You know, I passed this a dozen times and never saw this. This is brilliant."

"I know, right?"

"What are we looking at?" Noah asked again.

Duane reached over the desk and pulled the post card from the cork board. "This."

"Laurel Caverns?" Noah asked, confused, then his eyes widened. "Oh my God, Laurel Caverns."

"Not sure how this will work with all that happened, but," Duane tapped the picture. "Typically, winter or summer it's fifty-two degrees. No matter how hot it's been, something about it gives it a natural climate control."

Aya added, "And underground rivers."

"Water." Duane nodded.

"How can we be so close," I said. "And not even think about it? It's right here in Uniontown. Ten miles."

"That's the problem," Duane said. "We are going to need supplies. There's not a vehicle working. They've all been fried."

"If they're outside," said Noah. "I mean. Yeah, this was a CME, bigger than Carrington, like way bigger. And it released an EMP—"

"Whoa. Wait." Duane held up his hand. "You know about this stuff? I'm impressed."

Aya gave a nod to her son. "My science nerd."

"Okay, but I'm not," I said. "CME? EMP?"

Noah explained. "CME, Coronal Mass Ejection, is what the sun did on a massive scale. Like never seen before. Ever see the movie, *The Knowing*?"

I shook my head. "No."

"Not many did. It's an older movie. Anyhow, in it, a CME just scorched and burned the earth. End of the world. That's an exaggerated version of what happened here. Anyhow, right before everything happened, the power went out. That is an EMP, electromagnetic pulse."

Aya shook her head. "But an EMP kills all electronics. All cars."

"No." Noah shook his head.

"Yes," argued Duane.

"No." Noah chuckled then spewed forth without taking a breath. "That whole thing that once an EMP hits, anything running will stop and never run again, is a total misconception carried over from the eighties when they didn't know any better. Yeah, cars are basically electronic, but they're safe guarded. In fact, back in the early aughts, they did a test, simulated an EMP and seventy-two percent of all vehicles started again after they disconnected and reconnected the battery." He exhaled. "Only problem would be gas, but we're talking ten miles. Piece of cake."

He rattled off fast and knowledgably and I was kind of jealous about it. How did he know so much?

"So we just need to find one that wasn't outside," Duane said. "Work on that. You know the area. We need to get this water back to her family."

Duane was right. We had been there long enough, I had been away from them long enough. But the news of the caves were a good revelation. If we could find a vehicle, we could get my brothers there without making them walk.

"Noah," Aya said. "Stay with your brothers. I'm going to go with them to check on her family. They're not well." She looked at me. "Just give me a minute, I want to grab some stuff to take."

I let her know I'd wait. While she gathered medical supplies, Duane left ahead of us to get the water there.

That quick trip to the Rite Aid had proved to be so much more.

I was hopeful. With the water, the cooler place to go and Aya, maybe we all stood a chance.

102

NINETEEN

ONLY THE STRONG

It didn't take long for Aya to get what she needed. I didn't tell her much about what was wrong with my brothers, but I supposed she had already guessed. She carried two bags of saline solution and told me on the way to my apartment that she did a lot of intravenous therapy when she worked as an intern at the hospital.

I didn't realize how much cooler that back area of Rite Aid was until we stepped back out again. I swore the temperature went up even more. It was stifling and too hot to breathe.

Duane moved faster than us. At first, I spotted him, but his distance ahead of us grew.

I was glad, he would get that water there faster.

Talking was difficult, but it kept my mind off the heat. Somehow I knew it was just the beginning and would get hotter before it got better.

Aya and I talked about what would need to be done.

Ideally, we'd find enough vehicles to take everyone and the supplies we'd need. However, if we found even one, that would work. I didn't know much about cars, so when Aya said that they'd have to drive at night to lessen the chances of overheating, I believed her.

The heat was a lot for me, I could only imagine how bad it was for Sean.

Josh was strong, I worried about him but not as much as Sean.

"How are you feeling?" asked Aya.

"I'm fine."

"Listen, once we get to the caverns, we'll start that therapy on you. It will flush out your system. We'll hit you and Duane, I assume your mom, because she was with you guys."

"Did you see any of those sores on Duane?"

She shook her head. "Sometimes, when we're older, our thyroids can filter that radiation better than when you're young."

"So how come my mom is sick?"

"Is she?"

"She was throwing up pretty bad," I said.

"It could be the heat. Dehydration. A lot of things. We'll take a look."

"Thank you for this. For leaving your family to help us. It's nice to see a good mom."

Aya reached out and grabbed my arm, gently stopping me. "Allie, you say that as if your mom isn't."

I shrugged. "I don't know. She may have done some things at her work that caused us to lose everything. And she stole from Duane. He doesn't know. I do."

"What did she steal?"

"Water."

"I don't know your mom. But as a mom, she probably just wanted to make sure she had it for you. A mother will do anything to protect her kids."

"But we'd be dead if it wasn't for Duane," I said.

"And I'm sure, without a doubt, she knows and appreciates that. If she took his water, then he had all the water, right?"

I nodded.

"She was looking out for you. Don't judge too harshly. Not now, not with the way things are, okay?"

"I'll try."

"Good. Keep in mind, everything that happened before yesterday doesn't matter now. Only the future and staying alive."

"Okay."

We started walking again.

"Aya, I'm sorry I said that about my mom."

"I won't tell if you don't." she mussed my hair some and we kept walking.

When we approached my apartment grounds, Aya slowed down. "Wow, it still looks the same."

"As?" I asked.

"I lived here growing up."

"Really?"

"Hmm. Yes. Good memories. Then again, it's not where you live, right? It's who you live with."

"Um…not to sound bad, but I used to live in a six-bed-room house with seven bathrooms, a swimming pool and a maid. I'm gonna say it makes a difference."

Aya laughed. "I wouldn't want that cultural shock."

My building wasn't far, I no longer saw Duane. He had picked up his pace.

The second we opened the main door, Aya let out a 'whew.'

"Hot," I said.

"Very hot. Too hot."

"Is it the building or the weather?"

"A little of both I suppose, but these buildings were always like an oven in hot weather."

She followed me through the next door and when I opened it, I saw my mother. She sat between Sean and Josh.

Josh already looked better, he was sitting up, drinking his water.

Sean was the same-weak and leaning on my mother.

The case of water that Duane carried looked as if it were dropped, some of the bottles had been dented and the card-board bottom bent. A small distance from them, on the other side of our apartment door, my father lay on his side.

Duane crouched by him.

"Mom, this is Aya," I said. "She's gonna see if she can help us. Medically."

My mother nodded slowly, moistened her lips and her voice cracked. "Could you check my husband?"

At first I thought it as odd, why check my father when my brothers were ill? That was until I heard Duane softly call out, "Aya, could you come here?"

Something about the way that he said it told me something was very wrong.

With an 'Excuse me', Aya stepped over the case of water and crouched down, like Duane, to my father. Her hands touched upon him.

Her head lowered then lifted and she glanced over her shoulder at us, shaking her head slowly.

"What? What does that mean?" I asked breathlessly.

"I'm sorry, Allie, I'm sorry. He's gone."

Internally, I blasted a confused, 'What?!" and my brother Josh, sobbed out, "Dad" And scurried over to him.

I looked at my mother, her head only lowered.

My father was dead?

How could that be? How? How did he die?

"There has to be a mistake," I said. "He was stronger than Josh and Sean. How?"

"Allie," my mother called my name.

I watched Josh hover his body over my dad. My mother didn't move from her position with Sean.

"Did we...did we take too long with the water?" I asked. "Did we kill him?"

"Allie," my mother barked my name. "Your father felt it. He felt he was dying. He told me he just needed to stay alive long enough. He didn't drink any of that water, none. That's why he went over there."

"Like a dog, he went off to die?"

"Enough," my mother said. "We need to focus on your brothers now."

I stood in disbelief, my heart breaking. How could my father be gone? It just wasn't possible. It wasn't real? How could it be?

I inched my way to Aya. Duane stood, placing his hand on my shoulder. "I'm sorry."

"How?" I asked.

Aya stood as well. "He was severely dehydrated, his core temperature was high and his body gave out. It is extremely hot in here," she said. "No airflow. This hallway is a death trap."

And my father fell victim to that death trap. So fast, without warning. I replayed the last moments I saw him in my mind. He walked on his own, stammering some, but nothing that told me he was going to die in the short amount of time that I had been gone.

Why didn't I say goodbye? Kiss him on the cheek? Something. Anything.

I just walked away assuming I'd see him again.

I would never make that assumption again.

TWENTY

THE TRUTH OF THE MATTER

Duane had left to search for a car after moving my father back into our apartment. I went with him into the apartment because I want to see if the contents of our bedroom bins were still there.

We didn't have dressers; we had those rubber bins that stacked in the closet. Me, Josh and Sean all had one for our clothes. Our other stuff remained in boxes.

I wanted to grab clothes for me and Josh. Going to the caverns would take us out of civilization for a while and we needed clothes.

I packed what I could into a duffle bag for me and Josh.

As hard as it was to think about, I didn't think Sean would need clothes. He looked bad. He was barely moving and his breathing was strained.

When I came out of the apartment, Aya was examining my mom. She had an IV bag hooked up to Josh, and the bag itself was on an apartment door.

Like me, my mother had marks on her hands and arms.

Aya examined her while Sean rested on her. I sat down on the other side of Sean.

"I feel fine, other than being tired," my mom said. "How's Duane?"

"He hasn't let me look at him," Aya replied. "I haven't seen marks but that doesn't mean he wasn't exposed. Look," Aya said. "I need you to consume water. As much as you can. Both you and Allie. Josh will finish that bag in a couple hours and he will be good to move. I would like to move him to the Rite Aid before we head to the caverns. It's cooler there. It's not even noon yet. Those temperatures are going to get higher."

"What about Sean?" I asked. "Are you going to give him an IV bag?"

"Baby, I tried," Aya said. "His veins have collapsed. There's nothing I can do."

"We should move him."

My mother replied, "How? Walk him to the Rite Aid? To the caverns?"

"Duane and Noah are gonna look for a car, we can drive him."

My mother shook her head. "He's too weak to move."

"So we're giving up on him?"

Weakly my brother Sean spoke up. "Stop. Okay. Please."

My mother glanced at me gently. "Allie, he was on hospice before all of this. Please remember that."

I didn't want to.

Even though I knew what was happening with my big brother, that didn't mean I had to accept it.

Aya stayed for a while, she kept squeezing that bag of Josh's. A part of me felt she was trying to wait for him to get better and another part felt she was waiting on Duane.

We talked a lot about the caverns. Surprisingly, my mother knew them well. She went there a lot as a teenager. She did something called spelunking.

Funny word.

"What happens if we're not the only ones with this idea?" I asked.

"It's four miles of caves," replied my mother. "There's plenty of room for everyone. How much do we know about how long we will have to be there? There's a river that runs under it. We can get to it. I'm thinking that might be the best place to set up camp. The flow exit for the river will bring in light and some warmth. It will feel cold."

Sean spoke up. "And dark."

"Yes." My mother ran her hand over his head. "And dark."

"That cave knowledge must come from all that spelunking."

My mother quickly looked at me. "Allie, was that sarcasm?"

"Yeah, sorry."

"No, please, don't apologize. You haven't been yourself in a while, it's nice to have that back."

With Duane asking me if I ever smiled, and my mother making that comment, I didn't realize how long it had been since I acted my normal self.

"Looks like we have a lot to get packed," said Aya. "Lights. Along with food, blankets. Knowing my son, he'll have made a list already. A lot of that stuff was in the back of Rite Aid."

"I don't know Duane well," added my mother. "But from what I gathered, he probably has as well."

I felt Sean's hand rest on mine and I looked down at him.

It took all that he had to lift his eyes. "You're gonna beat this."

"So will you," I said.

He fluttered his lips. "Please. It's alright though." He leaned against me again. "I've been ready for a while."

They were words I didn't want to address or even hear.

I was glad when Duane returned because it took away from me having to respond to Sean.

"I have good news and bad news, which do you want first?" Duane asked when he walked in.

"Definitely the bad news," my mother answered.

Duane extended an object. As soon as it came into view, I saw it was one of those outdoor thermometers. An old one, about six inches, some rust on the edges and a palm tree design.

I looked down it. "108."

"I grabbed this from the Red, White and Blue thrift store, when I felt the temperature rise," Duane explained. "Yesterday we peaked at 103. It's five degrees higher and I don't see it stopping today."

"Which means," Aya added, "if it goes any higher, we'll die. The human body can't take more than that without its insides turning to scrambled eggs."

"I don't get it," My mother said. "There are places in this country where the temperature gets that high. Vegas, Texas, people live there."

Aya nodded. "This is a moist heat because all the water, all the rivers around us are evaporating. Humidity makes it feel hotter. Trust me, we can't survive much higher temperatures."

"It's a cool ninety-four at the Rite aid," said Duane, looking down at it. "But it's not dropping in here. One degree. That's it. I have reason to believe that this is just the beginning, that everyday until it breaks, it will get hotter."

"The heat will bring dry Thunderstorms," stated Aya.

I asked. "What are they?"

My mother explained. "A thunderstorm but the rain evaporates before it falls because of the heat. California has them all the time. Aside from human error they are the number one reason for wildfires."

"When there's a lot of trees, and it's dry, one bolt of lightning and everything can go up," Duane explained. "By that I mean fires."

"Well," my mother exhaled. "Is there really good news?"

"Yes." Duane smiled. "Noah found two vehicles inside a garage. They started, not much gas, but enough to get us there and to lug supplies. We need to work on the supply list fast, figure out how many people, how many meals, we need to ration, and we need to work on that stat. Hell, I saw that whole palette of Ramen noodles."

"There are thirty cases per pallet, I counted them," added Aya. "That's seven hundred and twenty packs. We could live off that and vegetables."

"There are fish in that river," my mother said. "That's an option, too."

"What about the Costco?" I questioned. "It's not far, if Rite Aid is stocked, I'm sure that is too. There's no windows."

"Noah and I talked about that," Duane replied. "We're headed there after we bring his mom back for the boys. The problem is...we need to go. Tomorrow if that temperature rises it will start to get too hot to drive. Tires will over inflate, pressure on the battery, the cars could overheat. It's not that far, but those cars were in a shop. We don't know what's wrong with them. If they fail, the only cool doable route is through the woods, following the creek that heads to the caves. We can't carry enough on foot to make it."

"So we have to leave tonight?" Aya asked.

Duane nodded. "It'll take fifteen minutes to get there and we'll need time to unload, but if we leave by three in the morning, by sunup we'll be inside and safe."

"Then that's what we do," Aya said. "We leave as soon as we can, as soon we have what we need."

I saw her look at the IV bag on Josh. It was nearly empty, and my little brother was magically getting better.

Leaving as soon as possible to avoid the deadly rising temperatures was the only option. But sadly, as I looked at my brother Sean, I knew it wasn't an option for everyone.

TWENTY-ONE

DECISIONS

My mother used a wet cloth to wipe Sean's face, to moisten his lips, cool him down. It became abundantly clear as everyone talked about leaving that Sean wouldn't be able to go.

He didn't have much time.

Any movement of his body caused him excruciating pain.

My brother was leaving us. A moment I knew was coming but was never ready for. I was so tired from not sleeping that I couldn't even think clearly.

My mother was not leaving him. She was adamant.

"We'll wait," Aya said. "We'll wait."

My mother shook her head. "No. I need you to take Josh now to the Rite Aid. Get him strong, take my daughter, save my children. I'll stay."

"We can wait, Connie," Aya said. "We can. Noah and Duane will get everything ready and we'll wait for you."

"I appreciate that," my mother said. "But here's the deal. You're a mom, you have to save your children, and I need mine to be saved as well."

Aya reached out and grabbed her hand. "I'll get Josh to the Rite Aid."

"No," Josh whimpered out. "No, I'm not leaving my mom. I lost my dad, I'm gonna lose my brother, I don't want to lose my mom."

"Joshie," my mother spoke soothingly. "I won't be far behind. I won't."

"But you heard the man, the heat…"

"Won't get me," My mother cut him off. "It won't. I'll stay in the woods and follow the stream. I know where it goes. I did it a hundred times as a teenager."

"How about this," Duane spoke up. "How about I stay with your mom. I'll bring her to the caves. Connie, I know you hate me, but I can stay with you."

"I don't hate you, Duane," she said. "I don't. I was angry because I couldn't do what you did. You were so together and I just worried so much about my kids. I'll be fine. I'm going to stay with Sean as long as I can and I'll be there. Take Josh."

Again, my little brother protested verbally.

"Baby, I will be there. I promise." My mother grabbed his hand. "Please. You and Allie go."

"I'm going to stay with you, Mom," I said. "I'm not leaving Sean. I'm not leaving you. We started this together. We'll see it through."

Aya exhaled heavily and I heard it.

"Both of you are sick," she stated. "Both of you. Your strength is not where it needs to be. I say we wait. We all go together."

My mother wasn't hearing it. There was no winning that argument. In fact, I knew she wanted all the discussion to stop. Sean could hear us. I could only imagine how he felt.

Did he know everyone was referring to waiting until he was dead?

What a horrible feeling.

Shaking my head, my mother looked at Josh. "I promise you with everything I am, I will be there. But I need you to go and get better, okay."

Sean groaned out. "Go. Please."

"See?" My mom said. "Argument over."

"Mom," Sean spoke with a crackling voice. "Go. Take Allie. Go. Just leave me."

"No, my sweet boy. Not even a consideration." She placed her lips to his head. "Time is short. Go get ready. All of you."

My mother held onto my brother so lovingly and I felt horrible. I felt guilty. How did I get such a bad conception of my mother?

I left to find water fearful that she wouldn't give Sean any. That she would let him die.

I had this evil person built up in my mind and suddenly I was seeing her differently.

The temperature was rising in that hallway, I could feel it. That case of water wouldn't last, not if we were using it to cool down and drink.

The decision was made. My mother wasn't going any-where.

Josh was bad. He cried and sobbed. First hanging on to my mother, then Sean. He didn't want to let his big brother go. He didn't want to say goodbye.

I could see the pain in Sean's face as Josh held on.

My little brother was still pale, still sick, but stronger than he had been when we found him.

Finally, he relented and left with Aya and Duane.

Aya promised to come back and check on us before she left, and Duane did as well.

Before long they would be gone. On the short trip to the caverns.

My mother wanted me to leave, but I left her no choice.

We would take that journey on foot together. It was only ten miles. She knew the route. Even though she didn't need me there, I wanted to be there with her and my brother.

I wasn't around when my father left this earth. For sure, I wasn't going to be away when I lost my big brother and best friend.

I didn't care how long it took, I would savor every single minute I had left with my brother.

With my mother I'd face the inevitable and the inevitable was that we would lose another member of our family.

TWENTY-TWO

ASLEEP

A weird twitch hit my stomach every time I thought about my father in our apartment. It just felt strange, and as much as I wanted to pretend he was somewhere else, I knew his body was in there.

I was so sad about my dad that I couldn't even process it. Then on top of that, we couldn't even bury him. We had to leave him behind to decay at a super-fast pace because of the heat.

Sadly, we'd have to do the same for Sean.

Sitting in that hall with my brother and mother, the fantasy part of my brain went into overdrive. I imagined Sean suddenly hitting one of his revitalization phases where he was moving, with no pain, no crushing headaches, breathing well and walking.

Then we'd be able to take him with us to the caverns. I kept thinking about how they hadn't left yet. Maybe, just maybe, Sean would get one last gush of energy.

We kept him wiped down, and like me and my mother, he wore a neck fan because it was battery operated.

I watched that thermometer hover around 105, it didn't drop at all until the sun went down and I opened both the main front door and hall door. Then it went to 100.

I finally got my mother to eat something. We shared a can of SpaghettiOs. It didn't need to be cooked, the can was warm. Duane had brought it to us along with other food.

"Make sure you eat and stay hydrated," he said.

Hydrated.

If I never heard that word again, I'd be happy.

In the last two days it was spoken all the time to everyone.

I probably drank more water since the event than I did in an entire year.

I wasn't sure how much it was helping or if it was more of a precaution. One thing I did know, those sores on my arms weren't healing. I was starting to feel them, they hadn't hurt before Aya pointed them out.

My mother said hers did as well.

Duane came to say goodbye, to tell us that Josh was doing better and he would see us when he saw us. He'd be thinking of us.

I wondered if he thought maybe he'd never see us again.

I walked him out and that was when I realized we needed to keep the doors open. It was cooler outside. Although it was still hot, it was somewhat tolerable.

"Remember," Duane told me. "Follow that creek. Stay close, that will be the last place that gets the heat. You know where it lets out, right?"

"Yes." I nodded. "My mom knows that way well."

"It's going to add two miles to your journey, and the terrain won't be easy, but you can do it in one night. Take only what you need. We'll have the rest."

"What if you get there and its full of people who won't let you in?"

"They'll let us in. Plus," he winked. "Your mom told us where that secret entrance was."

We said our goodbyes and I thanked him again before I went back inside.

I announced they were leaving when I took my seat next to Sean.

"You…feel cooler," Sean's hand rested on mine.

"It's cooler out. Then again, when would you ever in your life believe that ninety was cool?"

"When you're sitting in 110," Sean laughed, then coughed.

With a 'shh', my mom gave him water.

He sipped. "I want to talk to you guys. Please."

"About?" my mom asked.

"Anything. You guys didn't have to stay."

"We did," my mother stroked his forehead.

"We're not going without you," I said. "So you need to get better."

"You're funny," Sean told me. "We knew since October I wasn't getting better." His words were strained, croaky, when he spoke.

"I wish I could have made this better for you," my mother told him. "The old house had that basement family room. It was always cool, even without air conditioning. I loved that house."

"It's will still be there," I told her. "We can go back when this is done."

"Allie, I'm not sure this will be done for a long time. Not in my lifetime."

Sean jokingly added. "Not in mine."

"Sean," I snapped. "Stop. Okay. Mom, why do you say that?"

"Because even if the temperatures rise to unlivable temperatures for just a week, that's enough for a lifetime. I'm willing to bet wildfires have already started, all that smoke in the air. Temperatures will kill everyone exposed. The lakes, streams, oceans, they'll start to evaporate. On a normal basis, evaporation accounts for ninety percent of earth's moisture and water cycle. That's under a normal basis. Now add extremely high temperatures, evaporation will be exasperated, more moisture and water will go up than ever before. What is it that Duane said to you? What goes up, must come down? Eventually it will. We're talking floods."

Groggily Sean said. "More so from glaciers melting."

I looked at him quickly. "What?"

"Ice will melt, where's that water going to go. All that fresh water dumping into the ocean."

My mother added, "And we've all seen *The Day After Tomorrow.*"

"No," I shook my head. "No, we have not all seen it. Those disaster movies were a you and Sean thing. Every…" I stopped talking and turned my head.

"What is it?" My mother asked.

"You paid attention to us. You did 'Mom' things with us."

"Of course, I did."

"I'm sorry, Mom, I'm sorry," I glanced at her sadly. "I don't know why I have been so angry with you, forgetting things that I shouldn't have."

"I get why you're angry with me, maybe even your father," she said. "You have every right to be. You went from a privileged life to this."

"It's not your fault."

"Yeah, actually, it was," she replied. "The only good thing to come out of it was state care for Sean which was actually better than our insurance."

"How was it your fault?" I questioned. "I mean, like unless what Duane said was true."

"Duane said something about me?"

I shook my head. "Not exactly. About Norvo and things happening there."

"Embezzlement?" my mom asked.

"Yeah, I think so. Yeah, that's it. He said it could be they were trying to use that as a cover up for some sort of medicine error that his daughter died from."

"Oh my God," my mother sounded shocked. "Oh my God, I didn't know he lost a child. I am so sorry to hear that. That's heartbreaking."

I didn't comment on that, because I knew, before long, despite how much I wanted my brother to have a miracle, it wasn't going to happen, and my mom was about to learn what that heartbreak felt like.

"He did, medication from Norvo caused her death," I said. "He was the one that told me about everything. So he was right about the coverup? That they used you to keep the public from knowing about the tainted medication?"

"No, he was right about the embezzlement."

"Mom?"

"Your father and I took a lot of money from the company."

I felt a shriek of surprise coming from me and I stopped it, "For real?"

She nodded. "Sean knew."

I looked at my brother. "You knew and didn't say anything?"

"She asked me not to yet."

"Yet?" I questioned. "Were you going to?"

"Absolutely. After it was all settled," she explained.

"You and Dad really took from the company?"

"Oh, yeah, a lot. Our plan was to get enough to leave the country with you guys and start somewhere else."

"To get Sean cured."

"What?"

"You took the money for Sean, right? Because he got the same bad medication as Duane's daughter."

"Honey," my mother spoke gently. "Sean didn't get sick the same way Duane's daughter did. That was something totally different. It was children treated with epilepsy medication. Duane's daughter must have been one of them."

"Alright." I nodded my understanding. Surely she took it for good reason. "Still," I said. "You took it for Sean."

"No." She shook her head. "I took the money because it was easy to take and tempting. I started taking it years before Sean got sick. The timing just sucked. They caught me right after we learned about Sean's illness. Your father tried to take the fall. But they knew he didn't have the access that I had. I thought I'd get away with it."

"Do you have any remorse at all?" I asked, shocked.

"Only that I got caught and that you guys had to suffer. Allie, I've done this my whole life. I got greedy this time, really greedy," she explained.

"How did you not go to jail?"

"Oh, we were going to jail. We got a continuance because of Sean and I was working on leniency if we paid it all back. That's how we lost everything. They seized every asset we had."

Sean muttered out. "It doesn't matter now."

"I guess it doesn't," I said.

"Yes, it does," My mother stated. "I have to earn trust again. In myself as well. And I'm not off to a very good start."

"Duane's water?"

My mother nodded. "Yes, but I promise you. I will do better."

"It's a new world, Mom, as bad as it is, we all get a new start."

My mother leaned over my brother to me and kissed me on the forehead. "Thank you."

"You still don't feel guilty about that money, do you?"

"No."

I wanted to say, 'wow', but at least she was being honest now. Suddenly, as if in a snap of a finger, my mother wasn't this villain. She was real. She wasn't trying to hide behind anything. Everything made sense. How we went from living the high life to suddenly living a real *Schitt's Creek* Life without the funny moments.

It grew quiet after that conversation. For a moment, while we were talking, the heat didn't bother me, and I didn't think about what was happening with Sean.

My brother wanted to rest, and I thought it might be a good idea to sleep as well. But then the thunder started.

I wasn't sure if it was the dark and silence that made it seem so loud, but it vibrated everything.

Hints of lightning flashes came through the door, but that was it.

It reminded me of a summer storm, loud and violent, but no rain.

God, I wished it would rain.

Enough time had passed since they left that I knew my brother and the others weren't caught in it.

There was no way to know if they made it safely. It wasn't that far, they had to have made it.

The blasts of thunder came steadily, so much so, I had to go and see.

A part of me felt as if, like with any other summer storm, rain or no rain, there would be relief.

After telling Sean I'd be back, I stood and walked to the door. Outside that hallway door, the lightning lit everything, it seemed violent.

I walked straight to the outside.

The sky lit up with a firework display that only nature could deliver.

Bold and bright lights, horizontal lightning that ripped across the sky, illuminating the clouds in colors of red and white.

There was no breeze, no temperature drop. Nothing that even a summer storm without rain brought. No relief.

The air was oddly still and hot.

I waited and looked around.

The buildings were dark, only lit when lightning flashed.

It hit me right then and there, where were all the people?

Not everyone had died, they couldn't have.

If they heard the warning, they probably went below, but where did they go?

Other than Aya and her children, along with the man on the street, I had seen no other people after Large, Pa.

We couldn't just be it, there had to be more.

Yet, unless they found a way, the human race was destined to drop like every animal and human we saw out there.

Shriveled in the heat, boiled from the inside out.

As I looked to the sky, saw the desolate of the area around me, I realize my brother was right.

Nothing my mother did mattered.

Or did it?

Like she said, there was a level of trust she had to regain. I was worried. I really was. It seemed her thievery was a habit. An addiction she couldn't break.

But it was a different world

The repercussions of stealing millions were a lot different than the punishment for stealing water in a world that was dry.

Her taking money beforehand meant jail. Her taking water now could mean execution, because stealing water, a lifeline in the apocalypse, meant potentially taking someone's life.

I had been outside long enough and it was time to go back in.

My mother was sleeping, probably not deeply. Sean was as well.

"Man, it is crazy weird out there," I said as I took my spot next to my brother. "I've never seen it like that. The lightning is intense."

I didn't expect Sean to answer considering he was sleeping. How, I didn't know, between the thunder and that steady weird noise his neck fan made.

It rattled and snapped. It figured his was the one to break. Figuring I'd give him mine, I lifted the fan from him and shut it off.

The noise didn't stop.

It wasn't the fan.

It was my brother's breathing.

Gasping, I reached for him. "Sean. Sean."

His breathing didn't change and he didn't respond.

Slow…gasping.

"Mom. Mommy."

She jolted awake and looked. Before she could ask me what was wrong, she knew. I saw by the look on her face. She closed her eyes tight and whimpered.

This was it. This was the end.

I hated it.

How unfair was it all?

I closed my eyes tightly, longing to capture an image of my brother before he was sick, when he had hair that always needed cutting. He was fit and even chubby when he was younger, instead of the skin and bones he now was.

His coloring was good, not gray, he smiled and his teeth were perfect and white, not discolored from medication. That strong, healthy kid was crushed by an unfair sickness that I hated. His last moments on earth were spent in sweltering heat, no electricity, no relief.

"It's okay, baby," my mother said gently. "You can let go. You fought so hard for so long. Rest now. Daddy is there for you."

I tried so hard not to cry. But it was hard to stop.

My father. I hoped that was true, that my father was waiting for him with open arms. It was just hard to believe that if there truly was a God, he could be so cruel as to have my brother's last moments be so devastating.

We stayed there in that hall with Sean. My mother held him and I grasped his hand. We said no more other than tell him we loved him.

Which I did.

I loved him so much and he was leaving me. Leaving me in a world that now made no sense. One that he and I and Josh could have conquered.

But no more.

His breathing started to slow, sometimes drowned out by the blasts and cracks of thunder.

I wished the noise outside would stop. Just stop. I wanted to hear my brother. I didn't want to miss his last breath.

It didn't take long, and I didn't miss that last breath. Although it took all my attention to hear it. It faded like he did. It was without fanfare. It was quiet, a hush of peacefulness took over and he was gone.

TWENTY-THREE

FORCE OF NATURE

Two years before Sean got sick, my grandmother died. She wasn't old, she wasn't sick, but she had a stroke and died within two days. We were able to say goodbye when she was attached to tubes along with a machine that did her breathing for her. In fact, I was at the hospital when it happened.

We left after she passed away, the hospital took care of things, and a few days later we had a funeral.

It was a natural course.

But unlike with my grandmother, no one was there to take care of my dad or Sean.

My poor father was put back into an apartment. No burial or funeral.

Just dead.

And now Sean.

How does one just walk away from the body of someone they loved so much?

That was what we wrestled with. I didn't blame my mother; it was her child. Was she to just say, 'okay, he's gone, we can leave now?'

It wasn't that simple.

We cried, we cried a lot in the after moments following his death.

My mother sobbed like I never heard anyone sob before. It was filled with soul, an anguish I couldn't understand.

It broke my heart. Not only had I lost my brother and father, but I was now also watching my mother experience an unbelievable pain.

I wouldn't pressure her to leave until she was ready.

"Should we bury him, Allie?" she asked. "Is there a way?"

Of course, there was a way. We'd find a way.

I hated leaving my father in our apartment, it crushed me to think that we'd do the same for Sean. He deserved more.

Not that my father didn't, but it was Sean and my father would feel the same way.

We talked about it. The heat didn't matter, we'd find a way. Carry him out and put him to rest. Respectfully and not just leave him laying in that apartment hallway.

It was almost daylight, although knowing the exact time was difficult. I didn't have a watch and my phone had long since stopped working.

It was a feeling that the night was almost done.

The thunder had not let up.

It was relentless.

Anyhow, we couldn't leave until sundown. From my understanding, the journey on foot wasn't as easy as it looked on the map.

There were literally mountains to climb.

I didn't look forward to what the next day would bring. I thought after we buried Sean, we'd go to the Rite Aid and wait there until sundown.

I didn't even know if my mother could leave Sean. I worried about that.

He was her first born, and I was certain that held a special place in her heart. In that hallway, she just didn't let go of his lifeless body. She held him against her so tight, as if her love was enough to bring him back.

I understood that and I wasn't going to stop her.

Taking it upon myself to figure out where we would lay Sean to rest, I left my mother alone and ventured out of the building.

I thought about the playground, how most of it was sand. It would be easy to bury him there. Plus, it was a playground.

I felt morbid and hated myself for thinking about where I was going to bury my brother.

But it had to be done.

It was a violent atmosphere out there. The thunder vibrated the ground. I kept thinking of Josh and the others, hoping they made it and were safe and out of the vicious dry storm.

Before I even stepped outside, I could smell it.

A burning smell, like someone nearby had a firepit going.

I didn't think too much of it. The thunder blasted and flashes of lightning greeted me as I stepped out.

Veering to my right, the direction of the playground, I stopped.

Slowly, with a feeling of gut-wrenching horror, I turned.

The entire western horizon to my left was bright and it wasn't the sun. The sky was a brilliant orange that glowed and pulsed.

Lightning had struck and the fires has started.

I couldn't tell how far or near the fire was, only that it was massive enough to eat up the entire sky.

The plans to bury Sean, rest up at the Rite Aid and leave at sundown were out the window.

The fires raged.

The world around us was burning.

We were running out of time.

TWENTY-FOUR

DO WHAT WE CAN

When I told my mother about the fires, she looked at me with an expression that said, 'what else could possibly go wrong?'

She didn't say it, she didn't have to.

"Where did you see it?" she asked.

"West."

"You sure it's not south?"

"I'm positive. It's where the mountains aren't as high."

She slowly stood. "Not that I don't trust you, but I want to take a look."

"I understand."

"Stay with your brother."

Did she just say that to me as she walked out? Stay with my brother? Like he or I were going anywhere.

She was outside longer than I thought she'd be, a slight fear hit me that she wasn't alright. I was glad when she came back.

"You're right," she said. "It's south. No winds so it will move slowly. Nothing is blowing at all out there. There's still a lot of lightning."

"What do we do?"

"We need to bury Sean now."

"I was thinking about the playground," I said. "It's all sand. Not sure how deep it goes."

"That's a great idea. It's not too far to carry him either. Allie, could you go into our apartment, hall closet by the bathroom and grab me a sheet from the top shelf?"

I replied without hesitation or thinking. I said 'Sure' but regretted it the second I opened our apartment door.

How did I forget for a split second that my father's body was in there in that intense heat?? It didn't take long for the smell to remind me.

It was so bad. So absolutely horrible that I had never had my gag reflexes kick in that fast.

It was a warm backing smell, like a pie in the oven, only putrid and thick.

The retching was out of control, an enormous amount of saliva that I didn't even know I was capable of producing poured from my mouth before I finally vomited.

I hated that I was throwing up because of my father's body. When I finally felt my stomach calm down, I lifted my shirt and took a deep breath through my mouth, holding it.

The hall closet wasn't far, and I dashed my way there. I could hold my breath a really long time, so I imagined I was under water.

I threw open the hall closet and just grabbed the sheets from the top. I turned to run back out, still holding my breath, but this time as I crossed the living room, I saw my father.

While Duane didn't just toss him, he didn't cover him either. I suppose he didn't think about that. My father was positioned on his side, as if he were taking a nap. His face was gray and swollen and his tee shirt looked like it had blood on it.

I was certain it wasn't blood, because it was discolored, a water orange-brown, as if he spilled tea on his chest. He was so bloated.

He deserved so much more than to be left there to rot on the burnt carpet of a stupid apartment.

But it was what it was.

Even if we wanted to bury him with Sean, we couldn't move him. Something told me his body couldn't be touched. His skin seemed so stretched, tiny rips in his flesh appeared. It just seemed logical to me that with even the slightest movie, he could burst or rip further.

He lay on the floor near the window. The same window I sat at forty-eight hours earlier, trying to get a signal, while looking at the snow outside. Looking out, grateful that I didn't have to shovel the walk, talking to Sean and trying to learn about the solar storm. Never in my wildest dreams did I imagine how bad it would be.

For the most part, the apartment was destroyed. Flash burned.

I stood there for several seconds, just frozen, looking at what had become of my life so fast.

My father and brother were now gone.

Any home we had come to know was gone as well.

My mother, brother and I would be like nomads, moving from place to place to survive.

The same thing I was certain my mother looked down on Duane for when he stood on the corner hoping for handouts.

My chest hurt and I knew I couldn't hold it any longer. I was already pushing record time. With that sheet in my hand, I ran the rest of the way out of the apartment. Wheezing as I hit the hall and slammed the door.

"Are you okay?" my mother asked.

I wanted to reply, 'No, no I'm not okay, this sucks so bad.' But I didn't. I handed her the sheet and nodded that I was fine.

TWENTY-FIVE

DARK HALL

My mother hummed a song from the 1990s, but she didn't say what it was. She was in her own world, a sad one.

Another surprise emerged about my mother. In her purse she carried a small, travel sewing kit. I didn't know that my mother could sew, let alone that she carried this kit with her.

Not that she was creating a dress, she was closing a shroud that she made for my brother out of that sheet.

She hummed the song as she carefully wrapped my brother in the sheet, then started to sew it shut on the edges. She moved slowly, taking her time. It would be the last time she would see him, touch him, be with him.

I suppose in some way she was savoring those moments.

The last thing she would do for him.

With Sean's illness, my mother was prepared for him to go. I think she just didn't imagine this would be the way he did.

His funeral would be far from a normal one.

I felt useless and I knew how I could contribute.

"I'll do the grave," I said.

"What?" My mother looked up at me in shock, maybe even confused by what I said.

"I'll go dig it."

"No, honey, we'll do it together. It won't take me long to finish this, then we can go."

"No, Mom, I'll do it. Take your time. Stay with Sean a little longer. I'll be back."

"How? How are you going to do it?"

"I'll go to Building One. Super's room, I'm sure he has a shovel down there."

"Be careful."

"Of?" I asked. "People?" I softy chuckled. "No one is out there."

"Take a water with you, please."

I reached down for a bottle, casting my eyes on my brother's body in my mother's arms. It was painful to see, and it still seemed like a dream.

There were three things I took with me when I left the building. The water, the small flashlight, and a pillowcase, which I tucked in my back pocket.

I left the building, taking a deep breath when I stepped out. It felt like I was breathing water, the humidity was so thick and hot.

I rattled off places on earth that were hotter and people survived. Iraq, Tibet, Death Valley. Although I was sure humidity had a lot to do with how well a body handled heat.

The red sky in the distance didn't seem to grow much, that was a good thing. It didn't get any better and I could still smell the burning. It still pulsed, and I tried not to think of the inferno that was causing it.

I took the short cut through the grass to building one. It felt crunchy beneath my feet. I didn't know if it was the heat killing it or if everything had died before the heat wave because it was winter.

There were already no leaves on the trees and they had dried out fast from the sun, which is probably why they were burning along with other things.

The complex was dark. Not a light or candle, I looked. There was a chance that people were in the hallways like us.

Where did they all go?

There was no way they were all dead. They had to be hiding somewhere.

The only basement was in building one and I wasn't even sure that could be called a basement.

It was six steps down to the Superintendents work room. That was mostly underground, an interior room with no windows. I was in there just once to buy a lightbulb from one of the maintenance men.

It cost me two dollars, my can of soda and a Snickers bar.

I didn't mind because it could have cost him his job had he been caught.

We had three maintenance guys. How they all fit in that office was beyond me. It was lit with yellow lightbulbs, it was dim and reminded me of some sort of horror torture chamber.

Arriving at Building One, I was hesitant. Perhaps it was gut instinct, but I was slightly worried.

I didn't fear the people that lived there, I feared what I would find.

Before going in, I stopped at the door and set down my water. I pulled the pillowcase out from my back pocket, flapped it out. When I did, I watched a sliver of dryer sheet float to the ground. My mother always had this habit of tearing up dryer sheets and putting them with the sheets to keep them smelling fresh. I didn't think much about that habit until I used the pillowcase as a facemask.

I folded it and tied it over my nose and mouth. It was thick and uncomfortable, but it smelled good. I reached down to the ground and grabbed that sliver of dryer sheet in case I needed it.

My own breath made it even hotter and harder to breathe, but all that went to the wayside when I went into the building.

The smell of the building carried to me. Strong enough to cut through the fabric and mixing with the smell of the dryer sheet.

It wasn't the smell of death, I smelled that with my father's body and would never forget that odor.

This smell was sour, like a dog kennel of sick dogs. The scent of every bodily function mixed in the hot air.

I pressed the pillowcase tight to my nose and walked down the stairs. I would have to pass the door to the lower-level apartments. When I did, I saw the door was open and heard a series of strange sounds, all strung together, meshed in a way that meant they were hard to pinpoint.

Crackling, squishing, and then then other sounds emerged. I tried to distinguish them. A weak cough, a whimper, moan.

I realized that this was where the smell was coming from.

It was stronger there. I had stopped and, in a moment that I knew I'd replay for the rest of my life, I swung out the flashlight to shine down the hall.

I stifled the scream that tried to come out.

The hall was filled with people making camp in the dark.

They weren't even fazed by my light even as it bounced off of them.

Some were burnt, the ones I got a good look at were covered with sores. Bleeding, reflecting the light. I watched a woman closest to the door cough, lean forward and vomit.

As I aimed my light to see how far down the hall people were, the light reflected off the window at the end of the hallway.

Unlike our hallway in Building Four, that lower-level hall had a window at the very end. An older basement style window.

The glass was still intact.

Those poor people sought refuge in a lower level only to expose themselves to elements carried by the sun.

Elements I had been exposed to as well.

I shifted my eyes down to my arm. Looking at those sores. They were getting bigger and deeper.

Would I become the others who had them? Would my entire body become enveloped by them? Questions I wished I had asked Aya before she left.

I thought back to my mother sitting on the hallway floor with my brother. How the sores on her arms were still the same, but she had new ones on her neck and cheek.

Did she know? Did she even care?

Looking at those people, I wanted to scream and cry. How much suffering had they endured? It was heartbreaking. Instead of going to them, I stepped back, withdrew the light, spun with my back facing them. I leaned against the wall of the stairwell, just next to the door and took a few moments.

Why did I even look? There was nothing I could do for them, but still it mortified me that I had walked away. I felt as if I was abandoning those people. Internally I struggled with selfish feeling that was less than human.

Never looking for people, focusing only on those important to me.

I was sorry I couldn't help them, but I was there for a reason.

I went down the six steps to the brown metal door and reached for the handle, turning the knob.

Locked.

"Shit!" I exclaimed.

Being hopeful was a mistake, I turned and turned the knob. Then I resorted to hitting it with my shoulder as if I could knock it down.

In my frustration I kicked it, grunted loudly and turned.

I heard the door open along with something else.

A click-click.

I had never seen a gun before in my life before that day, yet, when I slowly turned around, someone had one aimed at me for the second time in a few hours.

What had we become as people that so easily aim to kill or at least threaten?

This time it was Orlando, the senior maintenance man. He was a slightly overweight older man, though I didn't know exactly how old he was. I was terrible at judging age. He said once he was a few years from retiring. That could mean anything.

As soon as he saw me, he lowered the gun. His hand shook and he stumbled back, bringing his hand to his face as he released a sob.

I wasn't important to him, did he even know me? Why did he get so emotional?

"Are you...are you okay?" I asked.

Stupid question.

"Someone is alive and well," he cried. "I didn't think anyone was. I tried...I tried to help them. I can't."

"I'm sorry. I'm sorry you've been alone," I said.

"Did you need my help?" he asked.

"No." I shook my head. "I just need a shovel. I know it's a weird request, but me and my mom need to bury my brother."

Slowly his hand slid from his face, and he looked at me. Was it shock? Confusion? Little did I realize at that second that he'd be the help I needed.

He had buried his own family.

That was the story he told me as I followed him to what he called a good place.

He carried a shovel, only one.

"It won't take much," he told me. "I will help you."

"Thank you."

His wife and grandson were in his apartment when everything happened. They didn't listen to the news or heed the warning to get out of the sun.

By chance, Orlando had been in that little office working on fixing the security door pad for building three. His wife had sent him a text saying that people were in the halls partying or doing something.

Orlando didn't think much of it. Maybe the residents were having a party.

He needed to fix that security pad and then he'd deal with it.

The power went out, again he didn't think about it. The room went completely black and he always had one of those battery lanterns on his work table. He turned it on and finished that pad.

Maybe thirty minutes had gone by. He lifted his phone to tell his wife he was done, but not only did he have no signal, but his phone was dead.

The rest was history.

He missed the event.

He found those people in the hall all burnt.

When Orlando arrived at his apartment, the door was open. His wife and grandson were barely alive in the small hall by the front door. From what he saw, his wife shieled the small boy, but it didn't do any good.

He described them looking like something from the Pompeii museum.

They survived only another hour. In absolute agony.

At the time, he knew of one other person alive and unscathed.

Mr. Cramer, a man in a wheelchair who lived in the building, had taken refuge in his bathroom like my father and brothers and he was alive and well.

He was the one that told Orlando about what had happened.

And when Cramer learned about the fate of so many, he took his own life.

"And I used his chair," said Orlando. "I dug the graves and came back from my Martha and Owen."

"I'm sorry."

"I'm sorry about your loss as well. This way." He limped some, leading me beyond the playground. He was sweaty and hot, still wearing his maintenance uniform.

We stopped at an area just behind the playground. A treelined area. Some of the trees had been removed from the right-hand side of the patch.

Cleared for some reason.

In the middle of the clearing were two fresh mounds, next to that was a square dug up spot.

"We had plans to build a tool shed out here," said Orlando. "We dug up the dirt for foundation, but the snow came and it never got finished. It goes two feet down. Deep enough to bury loved ones. Still making the crosses, but I can make one more." He pointed.

After he explained about the hole I saw how it was foundation for the shed.

Probably ten feet by eight. His wife and Grandon's graves took up two thirds with a deep spot remaining.

A spot for Sean.

"It won't take much. I'll clear it if you want, then we can get your brother. Easier than digging a brand new grave."

"I don't know what to say."

"I think it'll be a while before any of us know what to say."

"Thank you," I told him. "Thank you very much."

"You go prepare your brother, I'll finish this up."

As Orlando moved closer to the graves with his shovel, I started heading back to our building.

I glanced back at him when I heard the shovel hit the dirt. Just thinking about what he was going to do for us, as simple as preparing a ready-made hole, it gave me chills.

For the first time, for a brief time, I had relief from the heat in the form of emotions.

Watching Orlando prepare the space next to his wife and grandson brought the reality home.

It was time to bury my brother.

TWENTY-SIX

THREE CROSSES

We carried Sean.

At the height of his illness, before the sun blasted away our lives, I don't think my brother weighed even a hundred pounds.

He was skin and bones, the cancer having eaten every but of him away.

He was physically fragile and light.

There was a bit of disbelief when I told my mom about Orlando being alive and everything else I had witnessed. Especially when I told her about the foundation ditch. As if I had some sort of heat stroke hallucination.

Then we brought Sean from the apartment.

I took his feet and she held under his arms. Which I knew had to be hard with his being sewn into the sheet. We didn't speak much, the sun was already bright in the sky and the temperature had intensified.

But the sky wasn't blue. Not like the day before. It was more gray, the sun poking through the clouds looking super white.

How odd it seemed to look to the south. The same place the night sky pulsed a glowing orange was now a hazy orange that covered as far as I could see. I wasn't sure if the fire was moving our way, I just knew there wasn't a fire by the mountain range.

It seemed like an eternity since Duane, Josh, Aya and the others had left. In actuality, it had only been seven or eight hours.

Surely they were there, making a home in the caves. Finding a way for the dark caverns to be light while breathing in the cool crisp air.

Each step I took carrying Sean was harder than the previous. He grew heavier and my heart pounded. And I didn't know if it was my imagination, but I felt sick and worn down. A queasiness hit my stomach and my head hurt. I couldn't be dehydrated, I was drinking plenty of water.

It took everything I had not to ask to take a break. I didn't want to drop my brother. My shoulders hurt and arms ached.

Finally as we rounded building two, half-way to the playground, we saw Orlando hustling our way with an empty wheelchair.

Please stop moving so fast in this heat, I thought. He was already breathing heavily before-hand.

"We can stop," said my mother. "Thank God."

"Why didn't you wait?" Orlando asked. "Here please." He walked over to my mother. "Let me. Sit in the chair. We will place your boy in your arms."

As Orlando took hold under Sean's arms, my mother let go and whimpered some. A sad, exhausted whimper.

She sat in the chair.

"Allie," Orlando spoke my name. "Let's carry him to your mother."

We did.

We brought Sean to her, resting his cloaked body into her arms. His upper half and head against her chest as his legs hung over the arm of the chair.

Together Orlando and I pushed the chair on the walkway.

"Do you need water?" I asked. "I have a bottle in my back pocket."

"Maybe once we get there. Thank you."

My shorts were baggy enough to carry that small bottle with me. Prior to everything, I wouldn't even let my mother drink from my water bottle, now I was offering some to an old man I barely knew.

But one who was helping my family.

We arrived at the gravesite and my mother cried briefly. She asked for a moment, pressing her lips to Sean and silently sobbing as her shoulders bounced.

I heard her whisper, "I love you. My baby, I love you." Then she nodded to us that she was ready.

The realist in me knew that one day I would bury my brother, but never did I think I would physically be the one doing it.

Orlando and I lifted Sean from my mother's hold. As we carried him to the grave, she stood and walked over.

We placed him down next to the smaller mound, Orlando's grandson. A pile of fresh dirt was next to the hole.

Crouching down, my mother brought her fingers to her lips, then placed them on Sean. "I'll head back to the hall, Allie. I can't do this."

"I understand, Mommy."

"I can do this," said Orlando. "I'll do this and finish the crosses. Would you like to say a prayer?"

My mother shook her head. "I don't think anyone has prayed more than me in the last year. I guess they were answered they way they should be." She rested her hand briefly on my face and walked away.

After she was gone, Orlando faced me. "I can finish this."

"No." I held out my hand for the shovel. "If you can finish the grave markers, I can finish this. I'll bury my brother."

A slow single nod and Orlando handed me the shovel. He didn't say anymore, he just walked away.

I stood above that shallow grave, looking at my brother's body tightly sewn into that blue sheet.

I had to remind myself that my brother, his essence, wasn't in that beaten shell of a body.

I pushed the shovel into the pile of dirt and lifted.

The first shovel-full I cast down onto my brother was the hardest. Emotionally and physically. Despite how painful the task was, I followed through.

I would move that entire mound over his body. It was difficult, but it was my way of saying goodbye.

<><><><>

The final bit of dirt had been placed in the grave and I was tired, overheated and dirty. I could no longer see my brother, he was just a mound, like Orlando's wife and grandson.

I wiped the sweat from my forehead with the back of my hand and looked at the sky. I wanted to see the fires, I felt as if they were closer and almost swore I could hear the flames. A broad spectrum of the sky had been taken over by the orange hue.

There was no way for me to know what time it was other than that the sun wasn't directly above me, so it was after twelve.

My mother and I needed to rest before we headed out on that long journey to the caves. While eleven miles really wasn't much, the actual journey there over the terrain would be hard in the heat.

We just needed to make our way to the highway and to the creek.

I wondered what my mother was doing. Was she getting ready to leave? We had discussed staying at the Rite Aid for a few hours.

Anywhere that was cooler than our building.

I began my walk back to Building Four.

"Allie," Orlando called me name.

I turned around to see him.

"I just need to know how to spell your brother's name," he said. "I want to make sure I have it right."

At first, I was confused, Sean's name was easy. Then it dawned on me that it could be spelled another way. I explained that it didn't have the H.

Before I moved to our building, I thanked Orlando.

"You didn't have to do this and we really appreciate it."

"I wish I could offer more," he replied. "Answers. I don't have any. Only what little I was told."

"Us, too."

"This heat will last a while."

"I know. We're supposed to go to the Rite Aid today. It's supposedly cooler there."

I cringed after I said that, thinking my mother was going to get angry for telling our plans. It didn't matter whether they helped us or not, my mother just seemed to not want anyone with us.

"Cooler is better," he said. "Before you go, stop by to make sure the crosses are alright." He said. "I am making them fast. I'm not a carpenter. But the graves will be marked at least."

"We'll stop by."

As I turned once more to walk home, I spotted the glow in the sky.

If that fire swept through town, the markers would go. Nothing would remain to let people know Sean was buried there. He would be like my father. Another body buried beneath the destruction of the land.

I felt bad for Orlando. A part of me felt he was being nice because he didn't want to be alone. I didn't know him well. I knew him, but not personally. He was just the guy that came and fixed the hallway light and our toilet that one time.

He knew our names. Then again, he probably knew everyone in the complex.

When I arrived back at the apartment building, my mother was already packing items.

She was ready to go. To move on.

So was I.

"These LED light will last a couple hours," she held up a long, flat light. "We can't use these until we get to the caves. We have no idea where everyone went in," she said. "My guess up top near the main entrance and visitor's center. But we are coming in below."

"Can we make our way up through the caves?" I asked.

"No. We don't have enough light. We may have to stay on the lower end until we cool down and then make our way up. We are going to travel through the night, but it will take us all night." She handed me my bag. "The water in here needs to last you. I doubt they left any behind at the Rite Aid. They may have since Aya told us to go there."

"If not, I'll make it last." I shouldered my bag. It was heavy from the water. "Hey, Mom. Orlando asked us to stop by and see his cross he made for Sean's grave. Can we do that on our way?"

I waited for that reaction I had seen since everything started. My mother's huff of annoyance and resounding 'no' to any suggestion that varied from what she wanted to do.

Instead, she said, "That would be nice."

The world had punched a lot out of her.

"How are you feeling, Allie?"

"Honestly? I don't feel a hundred percent. Not sure if it's the radiation or heat, or these sores." I lifted my arm to show her. "Just not myself, you know. How are you?"

"Same as you. We'll rest before we head out and then once we get to the caves we'll take time to heal."

"Mom, you don't think it will be too late do you?" I asked.

"I don't know. I hope not. But what choice do we have?"

That was true.

We gathered what little items we were taking. Traveling light was the best option.

My mother placed her hand flush on our apartment door and stood there for a moment. I believed she was saying her final farewell to my dad.

We left that building.

A place that marked a change in our lives more than once.

I wish I left there with better memories to take with me, the truth was, I didn't. It was a symbol of everything in our lives that we lost. From things like money that didn't matter, to my father and brother who meant the world to me.

Making our way to the gravesite, I could see Orlando standing there.

He looked down at the graves, his back to us.

As we approached, the three crosses came into view.

Newer wood. Each no bigger than eighteen inches high. It looked like he used one of those wood burning pen things to etch the names.

Under Sean's name was the year he died and age.

Seventeen.

I was wondering how he knew Sean's age and was going to ask, when I heard my mother sigh out emotionally.

"Oh, Orlando, thank you so much for this. Thank you."

"It was my pleasure," he replied. "He was a nice boy."

"And he always loved those power shakes you made him," my mom said. "Sometimes that was the only thing he could eat and keep down."

"It helped my mother to keep her strength. But this..." he pointed to the sky. "Nothing would work on a weakened body."

Hearing this shocked me. I had no idea that Orlando came over and gave Sean special shakes.

No, wait, it shocked me a lot.

Sean never mentioned it.

"You are such a kind man," my mother said.

Was this my mother?

"Orlando," she said. "Where are you going? You're not staying here are you?"

Hold on. Was my mother leading up to asking him to join us?

"What else am I going to do? It is cool in my office. Well, cooler," he replied. "Where are you going?"

"The warehouse portion of the Rite Aid," she answered. "Just to rest, then we're taking the creek way to Laurel Caverns once the sun sets."

"That is a really hard journey on foot."

"I know, but Josh is there already, along with others. You just follow the creek," she said.

"Oh, I know the way." Orlando gave a tired smile. "That is brilliant thinking. The caves never fluctuate in temperature and there is water. It's dark, but it's life."

My mother nodded. "Come with us."

My eyes widened. She did. She asked him. She showed true kindness to him when, for the last couple of days, she had been horrible.

"I'll stay here."

"Orlando, no. The temperature is going to rise. That fire..." she pointed. "Will make it here."

"You don't need to drag a seventy-four-year-old man along with you," he said. "You two are young."

"We're sick," my mother said. "We both were out too much in the sun. Radiation. There's medication at the caves waiting on us. So in essence, you're healthier than us. We need you." She looked over at me.

Did she see the shock on my face?

I shifted my eyes to him. "Please come. Plus, you know, we're starting things over. You know a lot of things that life taught you. We really need you."

He wiped his head again. "Alright. Thank you. I will join you. But if I get too much, leave me."

My mother waved out her hand. "You won't. If we get too much—"

"I will not leave you." He cut her off.

Orlando had a few things he wanted to do first and get. He said he'd meet us at the Rite Aid.

I still wasn't convinced that he was coming, or that my mother was in the right frame of mind when she asked him. Maybe it was just strangers she didn't take to.

It was time to go to the Rite Aid to rest for the journey.

I took one more look at the three crosses, and mentally said my final goodbye to my brother.

TWENTY-SEVEN

RUSTLING WATER

When I was eight, I was so sick. It was some sort of bug. I don't remember exactly what I felt like, only that I was in bed. The reason I remember that I was eight was because I had to miss my first communion. I remember staring at my communion dress hanging on the back of my closet. The night before my mother had made a few adjustments. I felt like a princess, and funnily enough, my second-grade self kept saying I was Princess Virgin Mary.

Ah, the product of Catholic school.

I felt fine when I went to bed, my mother and grandmother were getting food ready for the big party and I was so excited.

I'm not sure when I started getting sick, but my memory takes me to that bed, staring at the dress, feeling more poorly over missing the big event.

My parents still had the party for me. I watched from my bedroom window. People brought communion cards and presents.

I didn't blame then for having the party, they had all that food and the cake.

Father O'Brian came over the next day with Sister Mary Leona and I made my first communion from my room. It was after that my mother gave me the cards.

160

That memory came up because I felt horribly sick after that nap.

My mother wasn't feeling great either. We both were sleeping when Orlando woke us.

He suggested we stay put and not leave, get our strength.

The truth was, we needed that medicine that Aya had. We wouldn't get better without it. No amount of rest was going to do it. Not in the heat, plus the fires on the horizon added a sense of urgency.

I wondered if he could pull one of those magic shakes out for me.

I knew that wasn't happening.

He did add some powder to the water. I wasn't sure what it was. It made my hands shake less and my stomach not as jumpy. My head still hurt, but water and some ibuprofen took the edge off.

I just wanted to vomit, somehow that would make me feel better, or so I thought.

Push through. I had to push through.

There were only so many hours in the night.

We had a lot of ground to cover if we wanted to get some distance behind us, I knew I wanted to because I wasn't sure how much longer I could keep going.

It hit me all at once, but a part of me believed I was so focused on Sean that I pushed down my sickness.

My mother moved slowly and when we stepped out, it didn't seem any cooler with the sun down.

The sky flashed with the lightning. It scared me because I knew we were going to the woods.

Orlando failed to tell us that the fire had moved closer. I could smell it even more and see how close it moved.

I thought of all those poor people suffering in the hallways of our apartment complex and anyone else, trapped in their homes, already battling the effects.

The fire would engulf Uniontown soon enough, swallowing them all.

Maybe they would welcome it.

What a horrendous way to go.

Something else that was horrendous was when I actually learned that following the creek wasn't as cut and dry as it sounded.

We had to go down a road, then climb from that road down a hill to the creek, but that wasn't the one that would take us to the caves.

There were three roads and three different water systems we had to follow to get there.

I saw the route when Orlando pulled out the map.

"I don't remember it being like that," said my mother. "It was a straight shot."

"From, Fairchance or Hutchison it was a straight shot," Orlando said. "Hutchinson took you to the northern base of the old entrance. It is not a straight shot from here."

"Tell me again," I stated. "Why we're not taking the bikes?"

"Can you bike up that last hill?" asked Orlando.

"No, but I can walk up that road probably better than I can climb up and over hills right now," I told them. "I don't know if I can. I feel really sick."

With his flashlight, Orlando stared at the map. "What if we bike to Fairchance? That's about five miles." He pointed. "Get the bikes there, take them down Elm to Shelton and follow that to the reserve."

"That's where the cavern waterfalls empty out, into that lake," my mother replied.

"Exactly. That road stops at the lake, but we can get in the caves there. I have a map of the caves," Orlando said. "Even if we stay there until you build your strength until we can go up top, there's water and it's cooler."

Why was it not the plan to begin with, I wondered? Maybe we were thinking of better days when my mother and I felt well or the trees had leaves, creating a shade that kept the woods cool.

In theory it seemed like the cooler way to go to avoid the heat, but in practicality those winter dead trees were like matchsticks waiting to go up and none of us were fit to face those mountains and hills.

I carried that thermometer and it teetered at one hundred degrees.

We fetched the bikes from the apartment complex. None of us peddled very fast and it was hard going up the hills—there were a lot of them. Twice, it got to the point where I had to get off the bike. It took everything I had to push it.

I had never felt so weak in all my life.

When I felt like quitting, I thought of Sean.

He didn't quit.

He didn't give up.

As much as I hated the climbs, I looked forward to the top of the hill. Coasting down felt so good, the breeze created by the momentum was a relief.

There was a strange, scary feel to everything.

It was the middle of the night, yet it wasn't dark.

The lightning was constant, cracking thunder. The sky lit up blue and red, like a scene from some Netflix series.

The sounds of the storm surrounded us but there was no wind.

Fairchance was a small community south of Uniontown. Rather, Southwest.

We didn't think much about the fires, we could see them in the distance, that familiar orange hue. Once and a while they looked like they were straight ahead, as if we were riding right into them.

Little did we know, we were.

I didn't think that was possible until we got closer.

The fires had arrived, they were on the outskirts of Fairchance. The smoke grew thick and everywhere around us glowed red.

I could actually see the flames. Before, it was just the color reflection, not actual fire.

The heat intensified and the thermometer moved to over a hundred.

It didn't take us long to get to Fairchance. We were fortunate enough that Elm took us out of the fire's path. It wouldn't be long, though, until it was on our tail.

We left the main roads and moved southeast through a residential area.

It was a scary thought going into the woods. How fast could everything go up?

Orlando stopped to look at the map again, charting our course, trying to keep us out of the trees until we had to venture in.

We needed to get to Shelton. That was the road we needed. It followed the creek to the reserve and the caves. But it was lined with trees.

I watched him peer toward the fire, then to my mother and me.

"We can rest for a few minutes," he said. "We're close."

"Where are we?" I asked.

He pointed on the map. "It's not even five hundred feet to Shelton. That creek is about fifteen feet down a small grade."

"You know the area," I said.

"Well, everyone does, when you grow up here," Orlando replied. "But sometimes, as you get older the journeys don't seem as hard in the memory."

I looked to my mother. "We're close, Mom."

"I know." She exhaled and lowered to sit on the ground. "Real close. I can hear the creek."

I didn't know what she was talking about. I wanted to correct her and tell her that was the flames she heard, but then Orlando stepped back from us and turned his head.

"We can hear the creek," he said with some amount of shock.

I asked. "That's a good thing, right?"

At first, he looked at me with concern, then took a few steps toward the sound and I watched his head lower.

"Orlando?" I asked.

"We shouldn't hear the creek. It's too shallow. I have never heard the creek. I'll be back."

I watched Orlando with his flashlight walk toward the treelined area. I didn't understand what the issue was.

Why did it matter if we heard the creek? I guessed we would find out when he returned.

The freaky weather continued. Every few seconds the sky would light up and a blast of thunder would rumble the ground.

Waiting for Orlando, I made my way over to my mother and extended my water bottle. "Here," I told her. "Drink."

"I'm good."

"No, you're not. I haven't seen you drink any water."

"So we're monitoring my water intake?"

"You'd do the same for me."

She took the bottle. "Yeah, I would."

"How are you."

"Oh, Allie, I feel so sick. I wish now I would have taken that potassium iodide that Duane had," she said. "Maybe it would have lessened everything."

"I don't know, I don't feel all that great either."

She grabbed on to my hand. "We're halfway there. Almost. Almost." She leaned in and kissed me on my cheek.

"At least we know Josh is okay."

"I'm certain now that they made it."

"Me, too," I said, not quite as sure as my mother. I didn't let her know that, so I moved the conversation. "It's so hot."

"Vegas," my mother said.

"What about it?"

"Remember a few years ago, Dad and I went?"

I nodded.

"It was a hundred and eight. My sandals melted. I was mad, too, I paid a lot for them. Obviously, they were cheaply made."

"Obviously."

"The reason I am telling you this is because we can survive this heat. The sun is not battering us. We can make it in this weather. We can."

"I know we can." I paused. "I'm sorry about everything Mom."

"What do you mean?"

"Sean. Dad. I'm sorry."

"Me, too baby."

My mother took another drink of water and handed me the bottle. As I grabbed it, I saw Orlando returning.

He was out of breath when he reached us.

"Is the hill side that bad?" I asked.

"Coming back up," he replied. "Going down, not so bad."

My mother asked, "Should we take the bikes down and follow the creek?"

"No." Orlando shook his head. "We continue to Shelton and take that. Listen, Connie…the creek is high."

There was a moment of silent staring between them, like that was a bad thing.

"High?" she asked. "Like how high?"

"Like at least a foot higher," he replied.

"How is that possible?" she asked. "Do you think there's a storm north of here?"

"Possibly. The water is moving pretty good. It's been a while since I have been at the creek. It could be normal now. It just doesn't feel like it's normal. It's rushing, which isn't normal movement for a creek unless there's a flood."

"Why is this a bad thing?" I asked. "I mean, we're in a massive heatwave. I would think the water is good."

"Water is good," Orlando explained, "but we need to know where it's coming from."

My mother looked at me. "It could be a storm north of here. We don't know."

"We don't know anything, we just need to keep an eye out," Orlando said.

"Are we worried about flooding?" I questioned. "I mean we're surrounded by mountains." I really wasn't grasping what the concern was. "Do you think the storms will get worse?"

"I don't think it's storms at all," said Orlando. "Mr. Cramer, when he was alive, told me the authorities predicted worse case is heat first. Dry storms, no rain. It's too soon for rain. That's just my thinking."

I chuckled. "If it's not rain causing high water then what?"

"Something bigger," he replied.

"Like?" I questioned further.

He looked at my mother then back to me. "Not sure." He took a deep breath. "Are we rested? Maybe we should go."

And just like that he changed the subject. I felt like I was this little kid they felt the need to protect from the truth, as if they were hiding something from me.

I accepted his silence and ending of the conversation. Gathering my stuff, I got on my bike. According to Orlando and his map, it wasn't far until we would be in the thick of the woods, on Shelton drive, following that rising creek.

Not long at all until we arrived at the caves.

TWENTY-EIGHT

THE BASE

Fire.

This wasn't a Vegas vacation. It wasn't a hundred and seven degrees, it was hotter. We couldn't dart into air conditioning, there was nowhere to hide. The climate from the sun's temper tantrum was bad enough, but the inferno that wanted to consume everything intensified the heat.

That outdoor thermometer stopped at one hundred and ten. The red indicator was at the end. It was full.

I didn't really need that thermometer to tell me that it was too hot to breathe.

It was night. The temperature should have dropped, yet it beat at my chest. It was as if I had my head in a hot oven.

Even under normal conditions and circumstances things would be hard.

But these weren't normal circumstances.

We had to abandon the road when the fire reached us. Flames and smoke whipped in our direction and we made our way down the hill to the creek.

Abandoning the bikes was the only thing we could do to lighten the load. The creek spread wider than usual, making it hard to see what we were stepping on. The water came to our knees.

I thought about Josh and Duane, how I hoped that were safe. It had been almost two days since they left. Surely they were there, worrying and waiting on us.

My brother Sean would never have made the journey.

Why didn't we have more warning? Why was it only a day's notice? No one had time to prepare. Although I wouldn't doubt that some powerful people or scientists had time. They just didn't tell us about it.

The world was dying.

I was dying.

At least it felt like it.

The smoke grew thicker, and Orlando started coughing.

It wouldn't be long before me and my mother did, too.

He took off his tee shirt, wet it in the creek and draped it over the back of his neck, occasionally bringing the end of it near his mouth.

I ended up doing the same, walking in my bra or not, I didn't care.

The water felt so good on my back, even if it was warm.

It felt like we were walking forever.

We stopped talking because the smoke would make us choke.

My ankles twisted as I stepped on uneven ground. Every step I took, my legs felt weaker.

But I knew it wasn't far off.

Almost there.

Almost there.

I repeated it in my mind. When the lighting flashed, I could see our target. The mountain. Every few minutes, every few steps, that mountain was closer.

Until we could barely see it.

No longer was it just black smoke that slithered through the trees, but an orange brightness surrounded us.

It was hard to determine if it was the brightness of a fire in the distance or if the flames were upon us.

The woods, the dark and smoke created an optical illusion.

There was a brief moment of total fear that I wasn't going to make it. All that walking. The struggle, the inability to fully breathe, the pain, and I was going to die.

I took comfort in knowing the smoke would get me before the fire.

My mother grabbed my hand and yanked me. Difficult or not we had to pick up the pace, we had to run.

How much farther? I only believed we weren't that far because there was no way my mother would push us to the limit if we still had far to go.

Poor Orlando. Could he push any further or was he done?

I kept looking over my shoulder back to him, watching him struggle to keep up.

Then he fell.

My heart dropped to my stomach when I saw that. I stopped running and my mother tugged at me. She was oblivious to what had happened.

A haze surrounded him and Orlando struggled to get up. He lifted his head, looked at me, then waved out his hand for us to go.

I turned completely and pulled from my mother.

"Allie," she called my name and coughed.

I wasn't going to argue or hear her say to leave him. I raced back to him. He wasn't that far back. I wasn't leaving him behind. We were either close to the caves or dying, and the way it felt as if my lungs were on fire, I was willing to wager on the latter.

I arrived at Orlando, he tried to scold me to go, but he coughed too badly.

Reaching for him, I braced under his arm and as I tried to help, my mother grabbed his other arm.

"On, three," my mother said.

We helped him to stand and the light from the close-range fires allowed me to see that his arm was bleeding from the fall.

My mother brought his arm over her shoulder, and she braced him around the waist, telling me to do the same. I did.

"You girls go," Orlando choked out his words. "Leave me."

"Don't be ridiculous," my mother barked. "Just move. We have you."

I don't know why but hearing her say that made me smile.

It was difficult to move on my own, but holding up the extra weight of Orlando made it even harder. We weren't running, but we were moving.

My heart raced and adrenaline pumped. The smoke thinned some. Had we made some distance at least?

Then I saw two round, white lights dancing through the smoke.

They moved and I heard a voice in the distance. I didn't recognize it, he sounded young.

"I see them!" he shouted. "Radio topside. We have them."

Then two figures cut through the smoke. One man, one woman. I recognized neither. The guy wasn't much older than me and the woman looked as if she were my mom's age. Both were dressed in heavy clothing, which made no sense in the heat.

They wore facemasks.

It was a relief to see them. So much so that every ounce of air escaped me and I felt my body collapsing and I wheezed and coughed.

"We got you," the man said.

The woman took my side of Orlando. "We have you, sir. Daniel, grab the other side," she instructed the younger man.

Once Orlando was out of my grip, I realized I was getting a lot of strength from him. I felt even more weak. "Mom, I can't."

"Yes, you can." She grabbed me and put her arm on me. "Push it, Allie."

"We have to keep moving," Daniel said. "Follow us."

My mother asked. "How much farther? Are we close?"

"Actually," he replied. "You're here."

<><><><>

At that point everything became a blur. At first there was a rush. I felt better, energized. I didn't look at it as a rescue as much as being guided.

We made it.

That last bit wasn't easy.

The creek ending flowed into a small opening not far from where they found us.

It was a climb, but not steep, at least it didn't seem that way until the last little bit.

My mother was behind me. Thankfully, because at the end, I started losing it. She physically pushed me at the last stretch. It took a lot for Daniel and that woman to get Orlando up the final hillside to the opening of the caves. It was steep. It was probably the easiest one to get to. It wasn't until we reached that opening that I saw how far we had climbed and got a look below.

The fires raged in the distance and weren't as close as they had felt. Still, they were close enough for the heat and smoke to kill us.

I could feel a coolness coming from the opening of the cave, a dim light was in there.

Then everything faded and I had to sit down. The ground was cool and soothing, I didn't want to move.

Voices became echoing and doubled.

The woman left Daniel with us, stating something about going to get some help.

I didn't see where she went.

Daniel must have noticed me looking around, maybe he thought I asked him something. Maybe I did.

"We lit a passage to the upper levels," he said. "It's still dark, but not black. Your eyes will adjust and we'll help you up the rough parts. It's a good twenty stories. We can take breaks."

Twenty stories? I thought. Um no, that isn't happening.

And that was all she wrote for me.

I was told by my mother and Orlando that I walked, only taking a couple of breaks in the hour journey to the 'livable' section of the cave.

I don't remember any of that.

Telling Daniel, "Yeah, no, I'm not gonna do that" was the last thing I remembered. Looking up at him and muttering those words.

I finally understood the words 'blacked out', because that is what I did. That was the last cognizant moment I had until I came to. The sounds of children laughing and steadily dripping water in the distance brought me to consciousness.

I was cold, laying on some sort of mat in a large open area of the caves. I had an IV line in my arm and to my surprise, I was surrounded by more people than I expected to see.

TWENTY-NINE

TUNNEL VISION

It was similar to that feeling a person gets when they wake up and a few seconds later, they realize they slept in for something super important. Only magnify that by a hundred.

A wave of panic rushed over me and I sat up.

I didn't know a single person, they were all lying on mats like I was.

Were they all sick?

Oh my God, where was my mother, my brother, Orlando? Did something happen to everyone I knew?

I was getting ready to jump up, rip the IV out of my arm and race about looking for my mother when I heard Aya's voice.

"Whoa, someone is finally awake."

I fought to get the words out of my mouth because it was so dry.

Aya saw my struggles and brought some water to my lips. "Easy. Drink slow. How do you feel?"

"My mother. Is she okay?" I asked, panicked.

"She's fine," Aya crouched down to me. "She wasn't out long at all. How do you feel?"

"Orlando, he was a man with us—"

"Allie, everyone is fine. How do *you* feel?"

"I don't know. Fine, I guess, not sick like I was. Cold."

Aya nodded. "It's cold in here, yes. You'll get used to it." She reached for my arm. 'Ah, yes, they're finally healing. This is good. Very good. You were one sick young lady when you arrived. We think we flushed it out though. There's no way to run any blood tests. Not right now. We can gauge by the sores, which are finally healing."

"We? Who are all these people?"

"In here? Sick like you. Radiation. Some burns." She looked over her shoulder.

"Where did they all come from?"

"Same place we did. We thought the same thing," she said. "Run for the hills…. Literally." She smiled. "There are others here. Others that were here, but…there's a lot to cover. Let's get you unhooked and then we'll get you moving again."

"Aya, how long was I asleep? I feel like it was a while."

"A week. We had to sedate you to get you rested."

"I'm so cold."

"I know. One thing at a time. Maybe we'll get you up to the gift shop, people go there to warm up."

"Not outside?"

"Not yet. Save the questions. One thing at a time."

I was pretty confused. I didn't realize how many questions I had until Aya said that.

One thing at a time.

She said she'd be back, she needed to get some things to unhook me. She left me the water, which I sipped. When I brought the water to my lips, I glanced at my arms.

They were completely covered with sores. From the back of my hands up past my elbows. Sores that were beginning to scab. When did I get that many?

But I felt better.

I was so focused on everything else that I never really noticed how truly sick I was until I wasn't.

But I was safe. We made it to where we needed to make it. Now I figured it was just a matter of waiting to see what the next phase of survival would be.

"This isn't helping," I said to my mother as I looked at the map outside the medical section of the cave.

"Right now, it doesn't. Give it a couple days. Learn it."

"I doubt it. I'll never figure it out."

"You will. It takes time."

Time.

Yep, it was hours until Aya gave me the go ahead to get up and leave. My mother came for me, and outside that part of the cave was a map secured to the wall. Like a fire escape route, written in red ink with an arrow were the words, 'you are here.'

I was familiar with the map. Having lived in Uniontown, I had seen it a million times. Heck, the exact one I was looking at hung on the wall in my sixth-grade homeroom. My teacher got it from the gift shop.

Looking at it always reminded me of a stubby carrot pulled from the ground lying on its side.

The right side of the map contained the root of the carrot where the deeper caverns ran. The left were the spouting leaves, each a passage in the cavern system. The 'you are here' was on the second layer of leaves, one layer down from the easy-peasy tour guide section.

But the map really wasn't geologically correct. The root on the right was actually the northern section.

That was where we entered the caverns.

From what my mother told me, most of the people lived there because of the water and because it was near a larger opening. Other than a means of escape, the large opening provided an airflow that prevented carbon monoxide poisoning from the cooking fires.

The caverns were nature's skyscraper. Levels upon levels now utilized for living.

It was a complete system of civilization that I missed learning about because I was out for a week.

My mother told me we had a little nook below with Duane and Orlando. Where was Duane? I was surprised I hadn't seen him.

I was ready to go down below to be with my brother along with Duane, when that guy Daniel showed up. He looked like a boy Scout with his green uniform. His shirt and pants both matched and he wore this explorer style hat.

He wore his name tag, something he didn't have on when I first met him outside the cave.

Or maybe I didn't notice.

Young people need young people, my mother explained, so she invited him to be the one to take me topside and tell me what I needed to know about the caves.

He showed her and Orlando around. He knew Laurel Caverns because he worked there before everything happened.

"I promise to take you back to where you guys live," Daniel said. "Your mom just wanted me to show you the upper levels."

I was still lost on what had happened, but because I was feeling better and he was there to be a tour guide, I accepted.

We walked up this path that had a steep grade, but not so much that I had to hold on. It was wide and the ground was smooth and slightly wet. It seemed fake to me, like it was made for the tourists. I even made that comment.

"It's not. It's natural from the water."

"Water?" I asked.

"Up here," he said, pointing to the top.

I could hear a steady dripping and when we arrived, we found a small pond close to the edge of the natural rock wall. Water seeped over.

"This caused the slick walk?" I asked.

"Not just this," Daniel said. "Over time, centuries. Sometimes water builds up from rain. Flooding and so forth. This right now is the highest I have ever seen this pool. All the water in the caverns feeds into Uniontown. Or did."

"Is it fresh?"

"I would boil it. Come on, this way. Are you okay to walk?"

"I am, thank you."

I immediately knew the design was manmade once we emerged to the gift shop. The temperature had become hot and muggy. It still wasn't as hot as outside though.

"So the temperature dropped?" I asked.

"Oh, no, it's still one fifteen," Daniel answered. "Just here, the cold from the caverns kinda carries up. Watch your step. There's a lot of broken glass."

The gift shop reminded me of my apartment, not destroyed, but parts of it were scorched. The cases were broken, and as we walked to the large window where the deck was located, I felt the temperature instantly rise.

Surprisingly, the deck wasn't destroyed. It wasn't wood either, it was more of a patio built on a ledge of the mountain that overlooked the area for miles.

"It's safe out here," he said. "Come on. We'll only stay a short time. It gets hard to breathe."

He was right. The air was thick and hot. I could see fog over what I believed was Uniontown. There was a slight mist of rain and the sky was dark, rain cloud dark.

"When I step out here," Daniel said. "I always think this is what the dinosaurs lived in. I don't know why, I just do."

"So has it been raining?"

"Steadily, yes," he replied. "But it hasn't made a dent in the temperature. It put out the fires that actually caused the rain. That's what Doctor Clemmons said."

"Who is that?"

"The lead scientist here. This…" he pointed. "Is how we saw you. By accident."

He pointed to this silver thing. Oval shaped with tow round circles. It was used to see thing in the distance.

Daniel explained. "We were out here looking at the fires, seeing how close they were and by chance we spotted you guys. Walking across an overpass with bikes. It was completely coincidental. We watched as long as we could then sent out teams to areas where we thought you'd show up."

"We would have died if you didn't get there."

"Nah. Just would have been worse off."

"So you worked here?" I asked.

"Yes, as a guide."

"Were you working the day it happened?"

Daniel shook his head. "No, the cave tours are closed until April. I heard about the sun thing, looked up what could happen and made my way up here. I figured I'd bring what I could and hit the gift shop and storeroom for all the lights. It was a lot of snow the day before."

"I remember."

"I figured it was going to be a trek up Skyline with all that snow, but…when I got to Skyline drive it was plowed."

"Is that unusual?"

Daniel nodded. "Yeah it is. In fact, all the route to the mountain was plowed and when I got here, I saw the plow and a lot of trucks. It was Doctor Clemmons and her team."

"So she knew how bad it was going to get?"

"She did," said Daniel. "She came up a week beforehand and when the snow hit, she had a plow clear the way for the rest of the trip. They knew for a while this was coming. They had a lot to bring here. They weren't sure it would get as bad as it did, but they prepared as if it would. That's what she told me."

"And they're okay with people just showing up?" I asked.

"It's not the military. She's a nice woman. Her son and two grandkids are here. There's enough room. I mean, we're making things work."

"Thank you for coming for me, my mom and Orlando."

"Your friend Duane was out there too. Eight people all together looking for you. If you were making it to the mountain, it could have been any one of us that helped you get here."

He played it off as if it were no big deal, but to me it was. I know I was dying. That was evident by how long it took for me to recover.

I had seen the medical bay, the gift shop. Now I waited to see where I would be living. Living for the long haul and for however long it took for the world outside to become habitable again.

THIRTY

NEW HOME

Daniel had said it was a seventeen story drop to my new home below and I wasn't sure I really wanted to be that deep in the mountain.

Holding a copy of the map that Daniel gave me, I tried to follow it. I couldn't make head or tail of it. It was frustrating.

Daniel showed me where everyone slept, where my family was. And I thought our apartment was small. Our alcove was a slight climb up. A wide mouth opening that went back about eight feet and four feet high. Enough to sleep in. It was dark.

No one was in the sleeping area of the caves because of how dark it was, and use of lights had to be rationed.

So everyone stayed below.

Way below.

Not that it was bad. Actually, the area was nice, just kind of tricky and spooky to get to down a steep path that nature supposedly created. I didn't buy it. Everything was too convenient in the caves. That steep path led to a bridge that I knew nature didn't make. The single walkway bridge crossed over a narrow stream. It was several feet below the bridge and didn't contain much water, until we followed that stream.

Not only did it widen, but that's also when I started to see the people. They sat on the flat areas near the edge of the cave. Most at a distance from the edge of the rocks. I saw a few people washing clothes. They were the only ones near the edge. Lowering buckets down the four or five feet to the water below.

Others ate, talked and were reading. It was a place they called the Valley.

"This is where everyone is during the day," Daniel explained.

And I could see why. The stream moved steadily toward a wide opening and the light from the day came in. It also was warmer down there, heat carried in from outside and the water that had risen in temperature.

A fire was lit near the opening. Someone cooked over it.

"It's probably the best place to be," he said. "It really is dark in the caves."

"Yeah, I know. Thank you." I spotted my brother, Josh. He was by my mother. She lay on a blanket while my little brother faced a wall as if he were on a time out.

After telling Daniel I wanted to see my brother, I walked over.

"Hey." I put my hand on his head and then sat down. "Are you in trouble?"

He laughed. "No."

I turned my head to my mother. "Mom, you okay?"

"Just tired," she replied. "Still fighting this thing. You'll feel the tiredness. It comes and goes. Hits you all of a sudden."

As if she needed my permission, I told her to take a nap and moved Josh from her blanket to give her some space.

"Maybe there's more over here," said Josh. He lifted his head to the higher parts of the cave walls, searching for something as he moved a distance from our mother.

"What are you talking about?" I asked.

"What I was looking at on the wall." He pulled out a pen flashlight and shined it onto the stone. "Yeah, look. John plus Mary, 1955."

I muttered a 'huh' then I noticed the black writing on the cave walls. Two names, a plus sign and the year.

"Here's another." Josh aimed the light. "CM Wills. 1983."

"Dude," I said and moved his hand. "Look at that. 1894. That can't be right."

"Someone wrote it."

"Yeah, like employees," I said. "Make people think people were in this cave writing on the walls. I don't think you can write on the walls."

"Actually," Duane's voice spoke behind us. "You can't."

"See." I nodded. "They painted this, right?"

"No it's carbide. The heat of the flames causes a permanent black mark on the wall," Duane explained. "Years ago when someone was stuck here, they realized this when it accidentally happened, and that's how they made marks to find their way back out."

"So all of these are real?" I asked.

"Yep. People came her for over a hundred years and left their mark. You guys should leave yours."

I chuckled sarcastically. "Yeah, like people will come in here after us. I'm pretty sure there will be no more cave explorers anymore. I mean, who is left to care?"

Josh barked. "You never know. Plus, there will be people in the future that will come in here, I'm sure of it."

"True." I had listened to Duane but not turned around to look. When I did, I was startled by his appearance. He looked different. He had shaven, cleaned up and changed clothes. I had only seen him when the world took a downward spiral. Sweaty and dirt covered. "You have red hair."

"Ginger," he corrected. "I'm a ginger. How are you feeling, Allie?"

"Okay. Better, I guess. Better than when we came here."

"Me, too," he replied.

"Were you surprised to see all the people?"

"I was," Duane stated. "I shouldn't have been. I mean, we couldn't have been the only ones with the great idea, right?"

"Right. What is this Doctor Clemmons like?"

"Trina? She's nice," Duane said. "Very smart. Brought a lot of people with her. She will answer any of your questions."

"Not sure how much they can tell us though," I said. "Since we're back to the dark ages."

"True, but they're trying. Using old fashioned techniques with charts." Duane said. "Not sure how that works."

Josh added. "They're trying to find a power source, too. Like using the water, but it's not moving fast enough, or something like that. They said something about car batteries. I think I heard her mention one of them was working on getting the generator running again."

I looked at my brother. "You talked to her?"

He shook his head. "No, she's scary. I sneak up there and listen."

"She's scary?" I questioned in surprised.

"No, she's not," scoffed Duane.

"She is. Wait," Josh said. "You'll see when you go up."

"That's a long walk."

He shrugged. "You get used to it. What else is there to do? Listen to people's conversations, read the writing on the wall and board games."

"You could go get fresh air," Duane suggested. "You know, one of the times you go up top? It's safe, just hot. Only you can't be out long."

"Where's Noah?" I asked. "Aya's son?"

"Fishing," replied Duane. "A few of them go out daily. They should have been back. They go out for an hour and hopefully get something."

"Aren't the fish dead?" I asked.

"They were smart enough to stay deep. I'll let you guys go, I have to go help Aya in the medical bay. I'll check back."

I nodded and returned my attention to my brother. Everything was still a whirlwind to me. I felt like a fish out of water, everyone had developed some sort of normalcy to the situation. I was behind because I had been out of it.

It didn't take long before I got really tired. Just as my mother said, it hit me all at once. I didn't want my brother to know, so I told him I just wanted to sit down.

He joined me. "You need water?" he asked.

"Maybe. In a little. I just want to sit."

"Hey, Allie?" he softened his voice.

"Yeah."

Before he said anything else, he peered over me to look at our mom.

"What is it?" I asked.

"Mom doesn't say anything. She didn't say anything at all about Sean. Nothing."

I did a double take over my shoulder to her then looked back at Josh. "You know he died, right?"

Josh nodded. "Orlando said he was sorry. I figured that's what he meant."

"Mom didn't say anything?"

"She was really sick when she got here, like you. And I didn't want to bring it up. I know she's sad."

"We all are, but Mom is incredibly sad. He was her son. She'll talk about him eventually. It's probably just really hard."

"Did it hurt?" Josh asked. "Do you think Sean was feeling it really bad?"

"I don't think he suffered too much, Josh. He gave out. He was already really bad when this happened. It just took the rest from him. He rested and closed his eyes. That's how it happened."

Josh leaned into me, putting his head on my shoulder. "I'm really sad about it. It hurts about him and dad."

"I know."

"I feel it. Like a pain in my chest when I think about them."

I put my arm around my little brother. "Me, too."

"I feel bad because I haven't really cried. Have you?"

"When it happened I did. Not as much as I should have.. Not that I don't want to," I said. "But we've been fighting other things. I'm sure Dad and Sean would want us to focus on other things instead of crying. Not to say we can't cry. We can. We will. I have a feeling we will. Because we're gonna miss them more than anything."

"I already do."

"Me, too." I hugged him tighter.

"I'm so glad I still have you and Mom. There are kids here who don't have that. They have no one. I'm scared, Allie. I'm scared of losing you guys."

"I know. I'm scared too," I told him. "I can't promise you everything will be okay. I can't promise that nothing will happen. I can promise you this. But no matter what, we will do whatever it takes to keep this family together." I kissed him on his forehead and felt my baby brother snuggle close to me.

It was as if he were five years old, just needing someone, and I held on to him.

"Whatever it takes," I said.

THIRTY-ONE

WASH DAY

January third. That was when it happened. Two weeks after winter had officially begun, just after seven inches of snow had fallen…it happened. It melted the snow instantly and transformed the earth to a desert, or so it seemed.

It happened when it was the coldest. When everything to do with summer was tucked away. One moment the world was gray from snow, the next it was bright and washed out.

I remember thinking how fast my life changed when we moved into the apartment, it was nothing compared to the seven weeks that followed the event.

Now I lived in a nook in a cave. My brother slept between my mother and me. A new normal, probably how families slept in caves back when that was the best shelter from the elements and beasts that were beyond the cave entrance.

I washed my body a lot, but didn't change clothes as much as I'd like. My wardrobe consisted of the few clothes I had thrown in my bag and what I could find in the gift shop.

At night it was so dark. Everyone conserved the candles and flashlights. There was a strict lights-out rule. Not that anyone would get in trouble for lighting a candle, but we were considerate of what we had.

It was so dark that you couldn't see. The kind of dark your eyes never adjusted to. All you could do was sleep. Every snore, cough, escape of bodily air echoed in the night.

We heard it all.

It became a white noise that you fell asleep to.

Sometimes I'd listen to an adult tell a story to a kid and that helped me sleep.

Entertainment was storytelling, throwbacks to days that were never to return. Board games were treasured because it would be a long time until there were more.

There were no longer three meals a day. Two snacks and a big meal. Usually, the big meal was rice and whatever fish Noah and the others caught. It was enough to fill my belly.

Doctor Clemmons had brought cases upon cases of food, but we rationed that. Those items were the snacks.

We had enough, but we wouldn't for long.

Eventually, we would be able to grow our own produce using hydroponics. But that would take a while. Doctor Clemmons also suggested that once the weather switched up, we could send out people to scavenge for food items.

Not sure why I didn't consider that it was still winter.

Doctor Clemmons, or Trina, as we all called her, kept track of the days. I remember when Josh said he was sacred of her, I thought it was silly. Duane dismissed it. But when I met her, I understood why Josh was intimidated.

She had to be the tallest woman I had ever met. She looked like she could have been a professional wrestler. You just don't imagine scientists to look like her.

Trina was tough, strong, she spoke with very little inflection in her voice. She was matter of fact. Duane called her even keeled.

Not many people intimidated me when I met them, but she did.

I was too scared to even ask what kind of scientist she was. Heck, I still didn't know. I actually didn't want to talk to her unless I had something important to say or ask.

Unlike the rest of her team, she never came down to the lower levels with us. Duane said it was because she was always working.

I didn't get what she was working on or how they could work, until they finally got power in the lab.

They had only had it a few days. An hour or so at a time, but I guess they saw something because it had been days since we had seen anyone from her team at all in the valley.

Things were changing. There was talk about getting teams to do food runs, trying to find something to store.

The weather was cooling and would continue to do so fast.

I didn't need to be a scientist to know that it was happening. The water was getting colder. For the longest time, for most of the seven weeks we had been in the cave, the water was like bathwater.

The rapid drop in temperature just didn't make sense to me.

Especially when I saw one small piece of ice float down the stream that cut through the valley in the cave. The stream used to move slowly, but now the water was picking up pace and had risen at least a foot.

I knew it was February, but it didn't make sense for things to change so fast.

It had been over a hundred degrees consecutively for a month and a half, how was there ice?

Finally, I had a question I could ask Trina.

"Where are you going?" Josh asked.

"I was headed up to see the smart people," I replied.

"Why?"

"Uh, I wanted to see if they knew anything new."

"Why?"

"What are you, five?" I asked. "Quit asking why. I'm going."

"Can I come?"

"Sure?" I shrugged.

"Go where?" came a voice from behind. I knew right away it was Noah, Aya's son.

Before I could answer, Josh did. "We're going up to see the smart people and see if they know anything new."

"Cool. Duane just went up. I'll go with you. I was headed up to see my mom."

"Okay, but let me do the talking," I said. "I have a really cool question to ask."

"What is it?" questioned Noah.

195

"You can hear it when I ask. Is everything alright with your mom?"

"Oh, yeah. I just want her to know that the lady is starting up school for the kids and she's doing math right now with the twins."

"What lady?" I asked.

Josh answered. "Miss Marlo, she wears the tied ponytail, brown hair. She teaches sixth grade math at the middle school."

"Oh," I nodded knowingly. "Hope she doesn't want to school me. I am over that. And by the way, it's not a tied ponytail, it's called a braid."

My little brother didn't really seem to care. The three of us began the walk from the sleeping area. Just as we left it, I saw my mother.

"Where are you three going?"

I pointed. "Up top."

"Okay. I'm doing a wash," said my mother. "It's my day. Do you need anything done?"

"I have like four things."

"Then they need to be washed," my mother said. "Are they by your sleeping roll?"

"Yes."

"Your underwear?"

"Mom." I cringed.

"What? Underwear. Everyone has them. Are your dirty underwear there?" she asked.

"Oh my God," I just walked away.

"What did I say?" I heard her call out.

I actually really liked the version of my mother that had emerged from living in the caves. It was like the uppity woman I knew had hibernated and woken up totally different.

She was kind and smiled, even though I saw the sadness that came through many times a day. It was a sadness we all carried.

The people in the caves were all special. I didn't know them all personally, but I knew them by sight. Mostly. Every once in a while, someone would pop up and I'd wonder how I hadn't seen them before. Sort of like in school.

We all prepared our own meals, it wasn't like a camp with a mess hall. Trina had someone control over the rations they brought, and the fish were divided.

Josh started fishing. He hadn't caught anything yet, but he'd get there. It made my mother nervous. I think mainly because she had a fear of water, having never learned to swim.

My father made sure we knew how, but Duane and Noah both assured her that they would watch josh when they took him fishing.

I could understand her worry. She had already lost one child. That was devastating enough.

It didn't matter how many times I told my mother that I would do anything to protect Josh, she still had that fear.

I never thought it would be commonplace to watch that I didn't sit up too fast when I woke because I'd hit my head on the low bearing rocks, or not be able to open a fridge out of boredom.

Aya and a doctor in the caves made sure all of us kids went outside for sunlight once a day. No exception, no excuses. It was some sort of disease prevention thing that had to do with lack of vitamin D. Aya must not have gotten out much herself, we hadn't seen the sun behind the dark clouds in weeks.

All things I never thought of. I had lived under an assumption of life. No matter how rich or how poor, the basic routine was the same.

Until the event.

Making our way up, I felt that something was off. The medical bay area was a wide, open space at the stop of the slick grade. The usual trickle of water on that grade was steady like a stream, forming a large puddle at the bottom that had never been there before.

The water came from that small pool at the top just before the twists and turns that brought us topside.

The sunlight that carried from the topside entrance shone on the water of the pool.

The pool now flowed over the rock formation that created a wall. I could see it as we entered the medical bay.

I kept staring at the water seeping over, reminding me of a sink overflowing from a faucet left running.

The bay had six patients. Unlike when I woke up, it was full. Now Aya took care of an elderly man and three people still fighting for their lives with radiation sickness.

One time she delivered a baby. It wasn't in the bay. The woman went into labor down in the valley by the water stream.

Noah ran to get his mother and she raced back down. It took all of three minutes. I didn't think that was possible.

I watched the baby come into the world.

My mother really misconstrued my expression, believing that I was in awe of the miracle of birth. When in actuality, I just kept thinking, 'Please don't let anything drip into the water.'

Gross, I know. Wrong…But hey, I'm a teenager.

After the healthy baby girl arrived screaming loudly as if she had something to prove, my mother said to me, "What an experience huh?"

"Yep," I answered.

"What did you think?"

"I think I never want to have a baby."

My mother laughed, thinking I was joking. I wasn't.

I was at the medical bay, but thankfully no one was giving birth.

"You coming?" Noah asked me, pulling me from my stare.

"Um, yeah," I answered with a stammer.

I followed Noah into the medical bay and Aya immediately saw us.

"Noah Thomas, do not tell me you left your brothers alone," she said with a scold.

"Not on purpose," Noah replied. "That's why I stopped by. They are now in school. Well, they're the first students. The woman with the braid…"

"Miss. Marlo," Josh said.

"Yeah, her," Noah continued. "Is teaching them."

"You came all the way up here to tell me that?" Aya asked.

"Sort of. I was coming up with Allie and Josh," Noah said. "Thought I would tell you and see if you needed anything."

"I'm good. Allie?" Aya called my name. "Are you alright?"

She must have noticed my attention was elsewhere. "Yes, Aya, thanks. Did you notice there's more water?"

"Yes, just because there's been more rain," she replied.

Maybe she was right. But Daniel did say that in all his years at the caves, he had never seen it as high as it was and that was weeks earlier.

I was probably just being paranoid.

Noah finished up with his mother and we made our way to Trina's lab.

I always liked going the way of the gift shop, it was going back to the way things were…Sort of.

Trina's lab, or workspace, whatever it was called, was located off the old gift shop in an area where real geologists once worked on rocks.

Again, I wasn't sure what they did. Actually, there was a lot I didn't pay attention to. Like how they rationed, why they had look-outs, the whole system really.

Funny how when you're part of a system and not running it, you don't question the hows and whys.

Perhaps that was just me.

I could hear the voices as we approached.

Just the tone of them, the way they meshed together at a slightly louder volume, told me my gut instinct was right. Something was off.

"Do we know when it was taken?" asked Duane.

"No," answered Trina. "That's the issue. It could have been an hour ago when we got it or last week."

Another male voice spoke, "That would be devastating."

"You think?" Trina snapped.

"Trina please," he said. "We're all trying to process this."

"So the problem is," Duane said. "We don't know when and how much time. Worst case scenario, this picture was taken a week ago. That gives us what?"

No answer and I realized why when Trina saw me and the others standing there.

They weren't hiding anything. That was evident when Trina looked around Duane and didn't immediately go hush-hush. "Did you need something, Allie?"

"Um, I was just, we were just coming up to see if there's anything new," I nervously said. "You guys are busy, we'll leave."

"No need, you'll find out soon enough," Trina said. "Come in. Take a look at these."

They were all standing around a table and parted when I approached.

Duane explained. "For the twenty minutes we had power, Connor," He pointed to him. I had seen him around but wasn't sure what he did. "Connor," Duane continued. "Trina's tech guy, was able to tap into a weather satellite..." he turned when Connor vocally scoffed. "What? Is that wrong?"

"Tech guy? Tapped in?" Connor asked. "Dude, that's what I did for a living. I logged in to the satellite system. I downloaded the latest images, but unfortunately we don't know when they were taken because I can't reach the satellite."

"See." Trina pointed. "All three of these show a huge storm front."

Before looking at the pictures, I looked at Trina, she wasn't treating me like a kid and that felt really good. I gave her a partial smile of thanks and looked down.

Not that I knew what I was looking at. I didn't. But it looked like a hurricane. "It's big."

"It's one of many." She pulled forth more images.

"But aren't we expecting this?" I asked. "I mean, Duane always said what goes up comes down. The evaporated water from lakes, oceans, and such."

"Very good." Trina nodded. "We think all this is because things have destabilized."

Duane explained. "Remember I told you eventually things would flip?"

"Yeah," I replied. "All part of correcting itself."

Trina nodded. "Mother nature wants things to get back to normal. Not this tropical hell we're in. Right now, it's not stable because a ton of fresh water has dumped into the ocean and ocean currents control the weather as much as the sun. The sun took it one way, the oceans will take it another."

"You mean cold?" I asked.

"Yes," Trina said. "For a lot longer than it was hot."

Noah muttered. "Ice age."

Duane replied. "Sort of, yes."

From my little brother came the statement, "Is the big amount of fresh water the melting of the glaciers?" Josh saw us all look at him. "What? I listened to Miss Marlo. She said that was going to happen."

"We knew it was going to happen," said Duane.

Connor spoke up, "As I said, we don't know when these were taken. Are we good here in the caves? Absolutely, they maintain fifty-two degrees no matter what. However, we need supplies. If the images are from today, that gives us a week to start sending out for supplies. Because once it starts, it won't get inhabitable right away, but it will within three or four days."

"You said glaciers, right," I questioned. "Melted, dumped into the ocean. Could they have moved?"

Conner tilted his head. "If it was 1985. There was a lot then. It's decreased. Wait. Why do you ask?"

"I saw a chunk of ice," I told him. "Not big, baseball size, in the stream down in the valley caves."

Trina looked at him. "I mean, it's possible right? Last ice age, warm temperatures caused them to break loose and because of their own weight, they moved south. We know this."

"It was snowing when that happened," Connor said. "Or so we believe. I don't know where the ice came from, that is really interesting. I just know if any glaciers moved inland affecting our streams, we'd have some serious movement. Rising water, increased current."

Noah said, "It has, the water is moving faster and is higher."

"Son," Conner said. "It would be much, much more, like…" he snapped his finger. "A flash flood on a scale that no one has ever seen, it would roll through here like-"

"Trina!" A woman rushed in, she was out of breath. "I just heard from John."

I didn't know who John was, but I figured he had to be on lookout. I never knew what they were looking out for, but it seemed like I was about to find out.

"What's going on?"

"We need to get everyone up from the lower levels now. Water is coming fast, it's flooding the area, like a wall," she said hurriedly.

Connor pulled out a map of the caves from under the satellite images. "The natural canal system was formed thousands of years ago," he spoke rushed. "It will pour into here through those canals. We need everyone to the level of the medical bay and above."

Trina looked at the woman. "How long?"

"He can already see it," she replied. "Not long."

My mind processed everything and I knew exactly what he was talking about when he mentioned canals. There weren't any special waterway indentations, it was caves themselves. The ones with the smooth ground that seemed fake. They were the ones the water had flowed through before. That was what Daniel had told me.

"What about getting them out through Devil's Dog and our Cabe's Canyon?" Connor pointed.

Duane shook his head. "They're narrow, low and if the water gets in there's no way to go. Best recourse is to bring them up tunnels on the right side of the main canyon."

"The stairs will flood, as will the rope bridge," Trina said. "Whatever you do, keep them close to the wall. Scale it in case the water comes."

Was it that bad? Surely, it wasn't that urgent if they were taking this long to discuss the rescue.

I heard the hiss of the radio from the woman that had rushed in, then I heard what I assumed was John's voice. "It's gonna hit hard and fast. It's like ..." Crackle. "A wall of water."

My heart sunk and Duane flew by me, followed by Connor and Noah.

I spun to Josh. "Stay put."

"Where are you going?"

"To get Mom."

"But…"

"Please stay put."

Trina said. "I'll make sure he does." She walked up behind him placing her hands on his shoulders.

After glancing back once more, I took off. I didn't think I could move that fast.

Three minutes.

I knew Noah could make it down to the valley in three minutes. That had to be enough time. If I kept up with them, I could be down there just as fast.

Noah pushed past Duane and Connor, taking the lead and moving fast. He knew the tunnels and caves better than anyone, except Daniel.

He knew when to duck, turn, slow down, and pick up.

The water was coming. I could feel it. It wasn't a matter of overreacting. I could sense the increase in the water that flowed under my feet.

The bridge was slippery when we crossed, and Connor tumbled down four of the stairs in that last pitch run to the final tunnels to the Valley.

The ground had been made as smooth as marble from millennia of water, it was easy to know which way it would flow and where it was coming from.

Without a doubt that pool, not far from the bay, would be a starting point.

The radios didn't work down there. We would have to be the announcements.

Would the sleeping areas be safe, I wondered? Some nooks were five or six feet from the ground.

Noah emerged into the Valley, crying out as he did for his brothers. "Job, Hamm!"

"We need everyone to come out this way!" Connor cried out. "Close to the walls. Now!"

I thought to myself, if I didn't know what was happening, would I even listen? It was a vague warning.

Duane faced Connor, "Work on this side of the stream, I'll take the other."

I followed Duane over the second bridge, the one that crossed the cavern where the stream flowed.

Duane yelled. "There's a chance the caves are going to flood. The water is coming and it's coming fast."

It was one of those moment where no one wanted to be the first to move. It wasn't that they didn't care, they didn't understand the danger.

"We should be okay here," someone said. "The water will cut through this." He pointed down to the stream.

"No, we have to go!" Duane charged. "Stay close to the wall as you do. Now."

I saw my mother, she was lifting the bucket and looked at me.

She took it seriously.

The alarmed look on her face told me she knew something was drastically wrong as she dropped the bucker and moved toward me.

Orlando wasn't far from her, wringing out his own clothes. He stopped what he was doing as well.

I wish, I really wish I had paid attention to everything at that moment.

To everyone.

But I focused on getting to my mother. I wanted to grab her hand and get her out. Not that she couldn't do it on her own.

"Orlando," I said as I passed him. "We have to go. Stay close to the wall."

"Your brother?" he asked.

"Safe up top."

Duane ushered people as I made my way to my mother. She wanted my help, or at least wanted me out of the valley. I could tell by the way she stared at me.

I moved to her.

She moved to me,

And it hit.

I heard the 'whoosh' first, felt the pressure in my ears, and saw the bridge splinter into a thousand pieces as the water just came in a rush like I never expected.

So high, so fast and thunderous, I turned to race for my mother when I was pushed back and slammed into the wall of the cave just as the water rushed by. It grabbed on to my mother and took her from my sight.

Duane dived straight in for her.

Only for a second did I see my mother before the water swallowed her and Duane.

Orlando had pushed me out of the way. His body against mine, I felt water against him pushing the uneven rock of the cave against my back. I screamed and screamed for my mother, looking over Orlando's shoulder as I freaked out. Occasionally I saw a tumbling person caught up in the wave.

The water was so close, it hit my face.

It just kept coming.

Stop, please stop, I mentally pleaded. I wanted to get out, get in the water, but Orlando held me back.

My mother.

My poor mother.

Swept up, taken…gone.

THIRTY-TWO

MOM

No.

It wasn't going to happen.

It wasn't going down that way.

The water was relentless.

It wasn't one of those situations where it seemed to last a long time when in essence it was over fast.

It took a long time for the water to stop.

Ten minutes it raged by us and all I could think of was my poor mother. Swept away. And Duane, he jumped in after her.

They couldn't be gone. They couldn't.

Orlando had saved my life, but a part of me wished he had let me go, because I would have jumped in after them.

When the flash of the horrendous flood had settled, water that was usually feet below the edge filled that gully to the tippy top.

"Mom!" I screamed as Orlando finally stepped away.

The opening to the winder stream and lake was underwater. I raced to the end, ready to dive in when Noah stopped me, first extending his arm, then grabbing my shirt.

"I have to go, I have to find my mom."

"Not this way. What are you going to do?" he asked. "Just jump in and swim? You don't know what's there under the water."

"I have to go the way they went. I'm not giving up on her."

"I'm not saying to," Noah stated. "I'm telling you to do it the smart way. Follow me." He stopped at Orlando. "Could you go and see my brothers up top, please?"

Orlando nodded.

"Thank you," I told him. "Thank you. Tell Josh I'm fine but don't say anything about our mom."

"I won't. Allie...Allie the chances of your mother and Duane being —"

"I know." I cut him off. "But I have to try."

"Good luck." He placed his hand on my cheek.

Noah led the way and I looked around as we moved. There were a lot less people than when we came down.

I only hoped they had made it to safety and were not like my mother...swept away.

Noah's flashlight barely made a dent in the dark.

But it didn't take long, a hundred feet and I saw the light from the outside coming in.

Another cavern entrance buried in the trees, up on a hillside.

When we emerged, everything was different. Trees had been uprooted, the area below us was truly devasted by the waters that still lingered.

I could see a clear and precise path made by the water and we made our way to it.

It just seemed different.

The temperature changed drastically. It was colder than the caves, and the first of a few snowflakes began to fall.

The once narrow stream, five feet wide and two feet deep, was four times bigger. We walked along it, following the flow. We called out to see if anyone heard us, if anyone needed help.

It was loud, the water still moved with an angry momentum. The sky was that winter gray, just before a blizzard.

"Mom!" I called out.

Then, as the water narrowed, we saw them.

Bodies everywhere.

Twisted and bleeding from the violent ride. Some were up against the fallen trees, twisted against them.

I didn't want to look but I had to. I was now looking for my mother.

The sounds of moving water and wind captured the moans and cries.

People were alive, barely but alive.

What were we to do?

"Anybody!" a voice called from behind us. "Is anyone alive?"

I spun around.

Connor.

It was Connor's voice.

"Over here!" I shouted. "There are people alive!"

"Allie," Noah gently called my name.

I watched for Connor, he responded. I hoped he had his radio.

"Allie." Noah called me again, only this time I felt it.

It went through me. A call of my name that said more than I wanted to hear.

I was scared to face him to find out why he called for me.

Slowly, I turned back around.

"There. Look." Noah said with a point.

Downstream fifty feet, I could see Duane. He hovered over someone one. His body going from delivering breaths to delivering life-saving compressions.

I couldn't see who it was that he was trying to save, but in my mind and heart I knew.

It had to be my mother.

In the short span of time it took me to run over, the snow arrived.

It fell fast but it didn't stop me from seeing or focusing on where I had to go.

Not far from the water's edge, my mother lay with Duane beside her.

"Come on," he beckoned. "Come on, Connie."

Down he went again, giving her breaths.

"Come on," he begged.

I stopped cold when I arrived, trying to catch my breath, trying not to let the sight of it destroy me.

"Mommy," I whimpered out, dropping to my knees by her.

Both she and Duane were wet to the core, caked in mud, but I could see how gray my mother was.

Her left arm was twisted and clearly broken. An abrasion was across her forehead and her eyes were partly open.

Duane was trying. He was giving it all he had.

I couldn't believe it. He had nearly died trying to save her. He jumped into that water without hesitation and now he was trying to reverse what I thought was the inevitable.

Grabbing my mother's hand, I brought it to my face, watching Duane try to bring her back.

I didn't want to lose her, I didn't want Josh to lose her. How would my baby brother deal with the loss of his father, brother and mother?

In my mind, I begged for her to come back, but a part of me knew she was gone. She was with my brother, maybe stealing a moment. Holding her son, healthy again, looking at my father in some heavenly reunion.

Was I selfish for wanting that to end?

I needed her. Josh needed her.

Come back.

I squeezed her hand, feeling how limp it was.

Then as I relented, realizing my mother was gone and giving up...she coughed.

She coughed violently four times, each sounding like the crack of a branch.

Wheeze, cough and finally she splattered water from her mouth.

Duane laughed. I knew it was a laugh of emotional relief.

"That's it," he said, rolling my mother to her side. "That's it. Cough."

My mother choked on the water, coughing violently to clear her lungs.

I wasn't sure she even knew what was happening. Her body was just in some sort of automatic survival mode. Her eyes weren't focusing on anything.

She didn't know how Duane had sacrificed himself to save her.

I was so unbelievably grateful at that moment. I hadn't lost her.

Caught up in the moment, I didn't hear anything else going on. I didn't hear if Noah and Connor found people to help.

I focused on my mother. She was gone, dead…but now she wasn't.

Life gave her a second chance.

Like it did with us all.

Just like the water, the weather and my mother, I realized that everything could change in a snap in the new world.

My mother's hand was once limp, a scary limp of loss, but now her fingers squeezed mine and she looked at me.

I realized at that moment, in this new life, I would never take anything or anyone for granted again.

THIRTY-THREE

RUSH OF FUTURE

From one extreme to the other.

When we arrived at the caves it was so hot outside that I couldn't breathe, and it stayed that way for a while. After my treatments for radiation, each morning I had woken up and stepped outside to breathe in the hot, muggy air.

Air so hot it could kill someone who breathed it too long.

That was it.

The way of life.

An oven of life. Even with clouds dark and gray, rain falling at a steady pacy, the temperature soared.

The sun controlled the weather, but in the process, it set the course for the oceans to take over.

One second I was hot, the next I shivered trying to get warm.

I didn't know which of them I liked least.

In the heat, the caves gave us a soothing cool, but when the temperature dropped, the caves warmed us.

There was no going out to get regulated.

There was no going out at all.

We had a few days though before it got to the point where we were trapped.

That day when the waters came, we lost twenty-seven people. Most of which we never found, swept away with the tide of water. Duane said the force of the wave alone probably killed some of them.

My mother was one of the lucky ones, washed to the side by the wave instead of carried away. Duane jumped in for her and grabbed her twice, but the current pulled her away.

A dozen people were washed to the side and lived.

No one was really sure where the water came from, it was all guess work.

It came, it destroyed and it kept going. It didn't recede. It was like someone had dumped a giant bucket on the earth and we just had to wait until it all poured out.

By the time we gathered the injured and began getting them back to the caverns, the snow was falling steadily as well as the temperatures.

The ground, however, was still warm. Seven weeks of sweltering temperatures worked in our favor with the cold.

The snow melted immediately, and the water dried up.

It wouldn't for long. Once we got everyone back inside, Trina and Duane created salvage groups. While they worked on settling those displaced by the water, we'd go out. Not to return until we had items to build up our supplies.

The lower caves would dry out, the water would lower, all in a few days, until then, we needed to stock up.

Not only food but clothing, gasoline, medical supplies, everything.

Four trucks would go out.

We didn't know how long we'd be in the caves, but we planned for the long haul.

We had to find all the useful items in a world that not only had been flooded, but burned as well.

It wasn't going to be easy, and time was running out.

The near drowning took a lot out of my mother. Not only did she develop pneumonia, three of her ribs were broken as well as her arm.

I felt so bad for her, as if she hadn't been through enough emotionally and physically. Josh stayed behind with her, as my mother sunk into a depression. I understood that.

So much loss, too much.

I was on a team with Orlando.

We were assigned clothing and blankets. That was to be our main focus.

We cheated.

We headed directly to Morgantown and to the Walmart east of there.

Orlando's exact words were, "I'm not pissing around with anything local."

It was a gamble to go so far. The truck they gave us only had about a hundred miles of fuel.

He was banking on the mountains containing the fire and it the flames not reaching Morgantown.

He was partially right. A lot was destroyed, but the part that we went to was not.

The highways, while littered here and there with cars, were easy to drive and we made great time.

Our vehicle was dump truck size and we spent hours in that store. We loaded carts and just dumped things in, taking them to the truck and putting them in the back in no particular order.

We'd have time to sort through later.

So many items were there in Walmart. We grabbed clothes, socks, underwear, and shoes. There were lots of boots and coats on the shelves, The world ended in the dead of winter. We loaded carts of canned goods even though that wasn't on our list. It wouldn't hurt.

We cleared the shelves in the over-the-counter medicine section and took three large containers of antibiotics from the pharmacy. The only thing we didn't get from Walmart were blankets.

Those we got from the Quality Inn. A half mile up the road on the way home from Walmart, we went into the motel and directly to the laundry area.

There were two giant carts stacked with linens. Blankets, towels, sheets. We rolled them out and smashed the contents in the truck. By the time we called it a day, I swore we couldn't fit any more in the back of the truck. It was dark and we spent the night in the lobby of the hotel.

It was snowing pretty bad when we woke up. Still, the ground wasn't letting it stick. We made it back up the mountain long before it became impassible.

We were the second truck back and what we had grabbed blew everyone away.

They were singing our praises, thanking us left and right. An old man and young girl kicked butt.

My mother, as sick as she was, told me tearfully how proud of me she was.

I felt good about it. It was the first time since everything happened that I felt I had contributed.

I wasn't just some teenager sitting around.

We hunkered down. The snow and arctic cold were coming.

I was happy all the teams found so much stuff. It would take months to go through and sort. But that was okay because all we had was time.

There was one thing we didn't find. We found clothes, medicine, food, gas, everything ... except people.

I didn't see one other survivor out there.

Not one.

I didn't want to believe they were all gone or dead, that we were the only ones left.

I refused to believe that.

There had to be others. Eventually, when we left the mountain, we would find them.

I was sure of it.

THIRTY-FOUR

BIDING TIME

Happy Birthday, Sean.

Exactly six months had passed. The day before Independence Day, which happened to be my brother's birthday.

He would have been eighteen.

Happy Birthday to you.

In my head I sang it, maybe even mumbled it while staring at the picture I had brought from home. A picture of our family. We took one every year on Sean's birthday. We always had a big celebration for the Fourth, fireworks, illegal or not. We made it about Sean.

Even though it was taken in summer, my mother used the yearly picture for Christmas cards.

This was the last picture taken. Sean had just turned seventeen. It was right before he got sick. He looked so good, smiling that golden boy smile.

He was sun tanned because he had gone on a boating trip with his friend's family.

Were we happy as a family? Yeah, we were. I wish I knew it then instead of viewing my parents and our family through teenage angst glasses.

Happy Birthday, Dear Sean, Happy Birthday to you.

I ran my finger over the image, looking at my brother and father. The family that was and would never be again.

My mother had given us all this four by six photo album to put the pictures in. Each picture we took every year as a family on the third or fourth of July. To see with a flip of a page how we had grown. Not only in height and age, but in family members.

I'm sure my mother envisioned spouses and grandchildren.

I had thought it was silly. Who actually printed pictures anymore? But now it was a gift I would be forever grateful for.

I wished and wished there were more pages.

But there weren't, and there never would have been a picture with the five of us again even if the world didn't end. Sean wouldn't have made it to his eighteenth birthday.

In a sense, the world ending saved my mother, because she had no choice but to fight. Had Sean died in a normal world, that world would have consumed my mother. There was too much to take away her pain. Booze, drugs. She grabbed them when times were tough, I could imagine how much she would drown in them if they were available to her after Sean's death.

Now she had too much to occupy her, and that buried the pain.

The pain was still there. It would be for a long time. She didn't smile when she talked about Sean, she teared up. Often sobbing in the middle of the night thinking no one could hear her.

A woman in the caverns had lost her own son at seventeen. She told me it was going to take a lot longer than six months for my mother to find a new way to be normal.

Normal.

It was funny how normal had already changed in six months. How it had evolved.

How we went from boredom, learning how to wash in a stream and waking up without banging our heads off the top of our cave nook, to routines. Jobs that kept up moving and occupied. Education for the young provided by Duane, Miss Marlo and Trina.

I started going to their classes, I learned a lot.

We went from 'every man for himself' to a true community. From preparing meals for yourself or family unit to being part of a big mealtime for all.

Story time, music time, and it was just the beginning. It was early and we would evolve even more.

From self reliance to relying on each other and not being afraid to ask for help or to reach out.

There were positives to the negatives, and I focused on those.

I had to because it was hard.

From extreme heat that almost took my life to extreme cold. The wind blew at night so hard, it carried through the caves along with the snow.

Ah, the snow.

It snowed steadily for months. Once it started to accumulate, it didn't stop. A hard crunchy snow that never softened because the temperatures dropped so far overnight.

Many of us went to the mouth of a cave opening to stare out, feel the cold so we could appreciate the warmth of our shelter.

Step out into snow that was so deep it would bury anyone if it wasn't so hard.

The hard and heavy snow weren't without repercussions.

The entire top of the mountain, visitor's center, gift shop…it was buried.

The roof collapsed beneath the weight of it and the days of going up to the gift shop look out were gone.

Trina and her team could still get to her lab because it was part of the cave. Anything that wasn't was gone. But she evolved like everything else. She went from never leaving that lab to being part of the structure and community below.

Around the three month mark the sun broke through. Every day it would melt a layer of snow and every night a new layer would come.

It was without a doubt another ice age.

How long it would last no one knew. Beyond my years and life. I guessed I'd not see another day without the cold and white.

We were progressing, much like the crops in the hydroponics along with aquaponics. The growth was hopeful and seeing it told me that life goes on.

We moved on and just like those plants, we would keep growing.

With the two births we were a hundred strong. I envisioned other survivors out there. Maybe they were in camps or farther south where the weather was tolerable.

For the time being it was us.

The losses we felt were massive. I would never see my brother or father again, but I had my mother and Josh. We weren't alone in our suffering, everyone in the caverns had lost someone.

It was something we all had in common.

Overwhelming grief.

That grief moved us and kept us going.

One day we'd genuinely smile and laugh again.

One day we'd step beyond the caves, raise our arms and embrace the fact we could be outside for longer than a few minutes.

One day…we'd find others.

Until then, we'd make the best of it.

It could have been worse. It had only been six months since the world changed. That wasn't a lot of time. Time would bring more changes, more evolution.

We were fortunate to be where we were.

It would be a lie to say I was happy to live in a cave.

But it wouldn't be a lie to say I was happy to be alive.

ABOUT THE AUTHOR

Jacqueline Druga is a native of Pittsburgh, Pa. She is a prolific writer and filmmaker. Her published works include genres of all types but favors post-apocalypse and apocalypse writing. Currently, many of her films can be found on Amazon Prime and YouTube

A single mother of four, Jacqueline is also a musician. She resides in a small town outside of Pittsburgh with her family. Of all her accomplishments, Jacqueline is most proud of being a grandmother. Her grandchildren reside with her and are the light of her life.

Jacqueline welcomes emails. You can reach her at greatoneas@gmail.com